GAMBRELLI
and the
PROSECUTOR

GAMBRELLI AND THE PROSECUTOR
Published by Château Noir Publishing
Copyright © 2014 by Laurence Giliotti
All rights reserved.

Excerpt from 'CHARLIE CHAN IN LONDON' © 1934
Courtesy of Twentieth Century Fox. Written by Philip MacDonald.
Twentieth Century Fox. All rights reserved.

Cover design by Rebecca Swift
Cover photograph: Rue Quincampoix, 1932,
by Brassaï (dit) Halaz Guyla (1899-1984).
© Centre Pompidou, Paris, France. © Estate Brassaï –
RMN – Grand Palais/Adam Rzepka.
Localisation: Paris, musée national d'Art moderne –
Centre Georges Pompidou
Crédit: Réunion des Musées Nationaux/Art Resource, N.Y.

Library of Congress Control Number: 201 5901008
Château Noir Publishing, P.O. Box 19110,
Boulder, Colorado 80308, U.S.A.

ISBN: print: 978-0-9909266-0-3
ISBN: ebook: 978-0-9909266-1-0

GAMBRELLI
and the
PROSECUTOR

LAURENCE GILIOTTI

Château Noir Publishing

Dedicated to
The Investigators

"Great detectives are extremely rare. I believe they are the products of thousands of years of evolution. Their abilities to perceive and understand cannot be learned or taught. We can only wait for them to appear. It is unfortunate they are so few, and even more tragic that fewer still ever find their way into police work."

Arthur Gambrelli,
Chief Inspector of the Metropolitan Police

Quoted from a lecture delivered to the
Royal Academy of Criminal Science, Vienna, Austria
16 February 1932

FRANCE 1934

THE TIMES

Nuremberg, September 4

Nazi Party Rally
700,000 at Nuremberg

The sixth Nazi Party rally, which began at Nuremberg this evening, is the second to be held since Herr Hitler came into power, and every effort is being made to render it an even greater triumph of grandiose stage craft than its predecessors.

A new railway station has been constructed at Nuremberg to serve as a terminus for the 525 special trains...

4 SEPTEMBER

Island of Q
Six nautical miles southwest of Toulon, France

ONE

Annette Cuomo was not capable of deception. As a child, no matter what the offense—a broken porcelain figurine, a scorched pot, a missing piece of fruit tart—the truth would be confessed. All the while, her younger sister Lisa would glare at her as if to say, *Tell them nothing. They have no proof. A moment longer and they will give up.*

No, Annette Cuomo was not capable of deception. For that reason she had practiced this scenario dozens of times in her mind and aloud. She had played both parts, her own and his. She had prepared herself for any reaction her lover might have to her soliloquy, to her lie.

Now she could stand it no longer. Had he been looking at her he would have seen her face and posture gradually betray her words. He could have watched her struggle to hang on, weakening with every breath. The one thing she had not prepared for was his silence.

"Say something."

What did she want him to say? Jean Michel Bertrand could think of nothing as he thought of everything. The night was suddenly still. His lungs were without air. The tiny kitchen was without air. Heat radiated from the stone cottage walls, surrounded him, pressing on his chest. The sound of the ocean swirling along the rocky shore caught his ear. The smell of the sea revived him for a moment then it was gone. He leaned forward, elbows on the rough wooden table, resting his chin on the knuckles of his closed hands.

"For God's sake Jean Michel, please say something … anything." Annette's lower lip began to tremble.

Bertrand looked at her. She seemed more beautiful and desirable now than before she had told him. Her dark hair pulled back, away from her face, as he preferred. "It accentuates the elegance of your neck and adds to the nobility of your face," he had once told her. The small bulb hanging above the table cast an amber light on her glistening skin. She was so tan.

He felt a tightening around his neck. Instinctively reaching to loosen his tie and shirt collar, his hand found only naked, sweaty flesh. He looked down to find himself wearing a loose-fitting pale green shirt, decorated with beige and white sea shells.

He remembered hanging his suit coat on the wooden peg next to the kitchen door. He looked past her. The coat was there. What had gone wrong?

Less than an hour ago he had arrived in high spirits, placed the bottle of champagne and the flat blue box on the wooden table. "A celebration," he had said. He bent to kiss her full lips. She turned her head slightly and the kiss found her smooth cheek. It was then he should have known something was wrong.

He remembered going into the small bedroom and throwing his tie and shirt on the end of the bed. He had turned to kiss her, press her against his naked chest, but she had not followed him. She had always followed him, talking, touching, and kissing him. His momentary disappointment in her absence vanished in his excitement to tell her of his decision. He took the pale green shirt from the closet, the one he always wore on the night of his arrival, and rushed back to the kitchen. Bertrand had news for her. He hadn't realized that she too, had something to tell him.

"First open the box," he said.

"No Jean Michel, listen—"

"Wait." He opened the blue box for her. Inside were three knives; a large chef's knife, a smaller utility knife, and a paring knife, all gleaming in the light.

Annette said nothing.

"Sabatier knives. The finest." Bertrand held the box for her to examine. She did not even look at it.

Hadn't they agreed that a proper kitchen needed a good set of knives?

She moved a strand of hair that clung to her face. That was when he noticed the tears welling in her eyes. For a moment he felt she understood what the gift of the knives meant.

"Now let me tell you my news. I—"

"Stop." Annette raised her hand and placed a finger against her trembling lips.

It was then that she had told him. Told him their time together was over. She had fallen in love with another man, a younger man. She no longer wanted to see him. Annette Cuomo no longer dreamed of becoming Madame Jean Michel Bertrand.

And now, what did she want him to say? Should he tell her that he understood? That he wished her well? That he wanted to kill her?

Why was he surprised? Jean Michel Bertrand was never surprised. Hadn't he always feared this would happen? Wasn't he the one that wished she would fall in love with someone else? Someone her own age, with whom she could build a life, someone who would provide her with the happiness he wanted for her. He had told her so several times in the last year.

It was she who had professed devotion to him. She cried when he mentioned she should find another, someone free to give himself totally and without reservation. She was crushed by the idea of it and through her tears proclaimed that he was the only one she could ever love.

Confusion and shock gave way to anger. Bertrand was angry with himself. Why had he waited so long to decide he could not live without her? It was his arrogance, an arrogance that allowed him to think a woman so young, so talented, and so beautiful, would be content to wait forever for a man twice her age to come to his senses.

He had been a fool. A fool to delay the inevitable decisions he knew he had to make.

And now should he tell her, confess that he had decided to leave his wife, abandon his profession, and join her in their cottage by the sea? It would serve no purpose to confide that insanity to her now. It would sound hollow. A desperate man clutching at the sky hoping to grasp the wing of a fleeing bird, he could not live with her seeing him that way.

There was nothing to say. He loved her. He had finally admitted that to himself. If she would be happier with another then so be it, to hell with his life.

Bertrand took the chef's knife from the box and held it in his left hand, the blade strong and shiny in the dim light.

"The blade is carbon steel; it will tarnish if it is not cleaned immediately after use, especially if it is in contact with citrus or tomatoes." He flicked the thumb of his right hand against the finely honed edge. "It is very sharp, be careful until you get used to its weight."

Her arms were folded across her chest. Her head was down so he could not see her eyes. Annette nodded as if she understood his instructions.

Her shoulders shook and her chest was heaving, but he could not hear her sobbing. As he watched her his anger returned.

How dare she cry.

She is the cause of this.

She is the betrayer.

Bertrand stood up and raised the knife above his head. In a swift motion he drove the blade into the soft wood of the table. She raised her head, her eyes following him to the door. He snatched the coat from the wooden peg.

On the path to town he turned and started back to the cottage. Then he stopped. He would never see her again. Tears streaming down his face, his legs weak, he stumbled in the dark. He felt ill.

Walking quickly through the lobby of the Parc Hotel, Bertrand avoided eye contact with the employees and guests. Inside his room he flung the coat on the bed and poured a glass of water. He forced the water into his mouth. His throat was closed. He could not swallow. The water, warming in his mouth, tasted of iron. It made him think of blood. The thought of swallowing made him nauseous. He couldn't get enough air through his nose. He was going to suffocate. *Swallow*, his brain screamed. He could not. He spit into the sink. Gasping for air, splashing cool water on his face, he struggled to regain his composure. It was the room. The room was too hot. He pushed open the windows, but could find no air. The room was choking him.

Fifteen minutes later in the hotel bar he ordered another brandy. He was light-headed after the first, by the fourth he was crying.

"She is wrong. This is a mistake. I must tell her. Tell her of my plans to marry her. She will understand. She will love me again," Bertrand mumbled to himself.

"Let it go," the barman said softly. "Have another drink and sleep it off." He dried a glass with a white towel then placed the glass on a shelf behind the bar. When the barman turned back, Jean Michel Bertrand was gone.

. . .

Annette lay on the bed in the darkened cottage. She held Bertrand's white shirt against her body and kissed the dark blue embroidered monogram feeling the raised letters on her lips. She stopped crying and inhaled his scent with every breath.

The sea breeze pushed through the open windows and stirred the curtains. The sound of the surf grew louder in the dark.

For a moment, in between the crashing of waves she thought she heard the kitchen door open.

"Jean Michel," she called. "I left the door unbolted, hoping you'd come back."

There was no reply from the kitchen.

Was the sound of the surf tricking her?

"Darling, forgive me. I lied only to protect you."

She focused on the bedroom doorway waiting for him to step into the pale shaft of moonlight that crossed the threshold.

She heard one footstep, then another. She was certain.

"Jean Michel?" Why did he not answer? "I can explain everything ..."

A large shape appeared in the bedroom doorway.

"Who is there?"

A man stepped into the room. In the fragmented moonlight she saw his face.

"You!" She gathered the shirt against her chest. "What do you—?"

"I want what is mine." Another step.

"I don't know—"

"I think you do." He stood at the edge of the bed. A gloved hand held the knife. "Let me help you remember."

THE TIMES

September 5

Unemployment in France at highest level since the War

The Minister of Labour, M. Marquet has addressed a note to the Prime Minister announcing that the number of unemployed receiving relief is at present at the highest level on record since the end of the War.

An appeal has been made to the Prefect of the Seine to expel foreign workers to make way for Frenchmen.

5 SEPTEMBER

The City
Six Arrondissements, divided into ten police districts
Population: 1,300,000
480 kilometers south-east of Paris

TWO

Gambrelli had not heard the phone ring. Only the gentle prodding of his wife's hand against his shoulder awakened him.

"Arthur, wake up. It's the Headquarters' switchboard," Marie Gambrelli said as she left the bedroom.

Sitting on the edge of the bed he shuffled his feet, feeling for his slippers. He pushed his foot into the right slipper while his left foot slid from side to side in the dark. Lowering himself onto his hands and knees he felt under the bed. He touched nothing. To his left he heard an extended exhaling of air and a yawn.

In the dim light he could barely see the massive head of his black Newfoundland, Odin, as it settled onto the missing slipper. He crawled to the dog's side and pulled the slipper free.

Odin raised a large furry paw and swatted at his master's arm, pushing it away.

He leaned forward, buried his face into the dog's neck and began to nuzzle him. A heavy paw landed on his shoulder and pulled him downward. Madame Gambrelli returned to the bedroom.

"Arthur, the phone," she said, holding his new robe.

He struggled to his feet, groaning with every move. His wife waited, kissing his cheek as he let out a final grunt. Handing him the robe, she followed him down the stairs to the parlor.

He picked up the receiver from the console cabinet and pulled it to his ear. The clock on the fireplace mantle read 4:15 A.M.

"Chief Inspector Gambrelli?" The operator's voice had a metallic ring. "Please hold for the Commissioner."

Following a series of clicks the familiar voice of Police Commissioner DeMartell came on the line.

"Arthur, it's David. Sorry to wake you, but there's a bit of a problem."

Gambrelli was silent. He rarely commented on statements of the obvious.

"Gambrelli are you there?"

"Yes, go ahead." He took a cigarette from a silver box on the console and searched the pockets of his robe for a match.

"The Provincial Police on the Island of Q have just arrested Jean Michel Bertrand, the senior prosecutor at the Justice Ministry."

"I know Bertrand. What is the charge... arrogance?"

"Murder. They suspect him in the death of a young woman."

"Murder? Really." Gambrelli ran his hand against the side of his head.

"Yes, never would have thought him the type," DeMartell said.

"We're all the type."

"I suppose that's so. I was —"

"Method?"

"What? Oh, ah, multiple stab wounds."

"Where?"

"I told you, the Island of Q."

"The wounds. Where on her body?" Marie Gambrelli appeared at his side and placed his notebook and pen next to the phone. He cupped his hand over the mouthpiece. "A match?" he said to her.

"Don't know. The information is sketchy. I was advised by the Chief Magistrate. Bertrand called him and asked that you be dispatched immediately to intervene on his behalf."

"Why me? Bertrand knows I have never cared for him."

"He's in trouble. Who would you request?"

Silence again. He also avoided responding to questions the answers to which were obvious. Madame Gambrelli returned with matches and ashtray.

"The Ministry will cover your expenses."

No response. He lit the cigarette and blew smoke at the ceiling.

"Can you be on the six o'clock train to the coast?"

He replied with a grunt, and tossed the dead match into the ashtray.

"I will have someone advise your squad that you will be out of town."

"I'll tell them myself."

"I will notify Chief Superintendent Wilhelm that you will be gone for a few days. I'll make it clear to him you are acting on my orders."

"I'm sure that will make him very happy."

"Keep me advised of your progress. I'll see that your messages are relayed to the Ministry. And I will call the provincial police commander...his name is Ormond...Major Henri Ormond, and tell him to expect your arrival."

He hung up. Marie handed him a cup of strong coffee.

"A little sugar and the last of the cream... Do you have to go?"

"Yes."

"When?" She asked, returning to the kitchen.

"As soon as I am dressed."

He crossed the large Persian rug to the dining room, holding the ashtray in one hand and the coffee cup in the other. From the corner of his mouth the cigarette dangled. He fixed his eyes on the cup as the coffee swirled ever closer to breaching the rim. Remembering an old waiter's trick from his youth, he took his eyes from the cup and stared straight ahead at the dining room table. His peripheral vision assured him the rising tide of coffee had retreated.

The cigarette ash had grown long enough to curve downward. He tilted his head back to compensate for the bow in the ash and willed it not to fall. Forgetting about the coffee, he addressed this new concern by walking more slowly. He held the ashtray just beneath his chin, should the hot ash break free.

As if he were balancing a ball on the end of his nose he eased into a dining room chair. He felt a sense of accomplishment in defeating gravity's pull against the curving ash. He set the cup and the ashtray on the table. As his thick fingers touched the edge of the cigarette the ash broke free and landed on the lap of his robe.

"*Merde,*" he said, picking up the ashtray.

"Is something wrong?" Marie called from the kitchen.

He used his free hand to coax the fallen ash from his lap into the ashtray. His heavy hand failed at the delicate task and succeeded only in grinding the ashes into the cloth.

"*Zut alors!*"

"Arthur what are you doing?" She stepped through the kitchen doorway and walked toward him.

"Nothing." He set the enemy cigarette in the ashtray and sipped the coffee. "I have to get going."

"But you've only just gotten to bed. You need more than three hours sleep." She stroked the bristled gray hair on the top of his head.

"I have to pack," he said, brushing at the dark smudge on his robe.

"Pack? Where are you going?"

"The Island of Q."

"Now?" She didn't wait for an answer. "Why is it always you? You're ready to retire, for heaven's sake, and they are still calling you out at all hours of the night. Can't they find someone else for once?"

Gambrelli smiled. Neither of them expected him to answer. Marie seemed to be trying to repress a smile of her own. She shrugged her shoulders, and shook her head.

"I'll fix you something to eat before you go." She started back to the kitchen.

"Don't bother. I'll get something at the station before boarding the train." The brasserie at Central Station sold excellent croissants.

"So what is it this time that requires you to set out in the middle of the night?"

"Murder."

"And?" She stood at the side of the table.

"And the Provincial Police have arrested Jean Michel Bertrand for the killing."

"Bertrand the prosecutor? The one you call 'the peacock?'"

"The peacock is Branson. The detectives call Bertrand 'the Baron.'" He reached for the cigarette in the ashtray.

"So disrespectful."

"It's a new age my dear. The monarchists and civility have faded. Although, sometimes I wish for their return, just to put an end to the constant shifting of government."

"And if the monarchy returned, how long would it be before you found yourself at the barricades shaking your fist and waving the tricolore?"

"I may not be the republican I have led you to believe."

"Do you think he is guilty?" She asked, ignoring his attempt at humor, which as usual was solely for his own amusement.

"I have no idea."

"Who has been killed?"

"A woman. That's all I know." he said in a tone signifying the end of the conversation.

Not to be deterred she continued, "A prosecutor, and Bertrand no less. He and his wife are always in the society pages: charity balls, dinners, museum openings. I can't believe it." She took his cup to the kitchen.

"'Front seldom tell truth.'" Gambrelli mumbled.

"What was that?" She returned with a full cup, setting it in front of him.

"'Front seldom tell truth. To know occupants of house always look in backyard.'" He picked up the cup. "Remember, the Chinese detective from the movie the other night?"

"Now you're going to start quoting Charlie Chan?" She pushed against the side of his head.

"I'm considering it."

"Would you like me to pack while you shave?"

"No. Go back to bed, rest, and finish my dream for me. I was just about to kick a winning goal against the Austrians." He kissed her on the cheek and patted her shoulder.

"How long will you be gone?"

"A few days at most."

He watched her start up the staircase, sipped the coffee and put out the trouble-making cigarette.

THREE

He refilled the cup, placed the empty coffee pot in the sink, and turned off the kitchen light. He paused in the silence of the dining room. Soon he heard the gentle tapping of rain on the windows. He set the cup on the edge of the table. Through the balcony doors he watched the fog drift up from the banks of the Rhône engulfing street lamps along Boulevard des Belges turning the dim lights into clouds of faded gold in the dark. The mist was thick and shrouded the trees inside the gates of the Parc de la Tête D'Or across the boulevard.

He knew Marie was upstairs. Had she already returned to sleep surrounded by the warmth of the bed? The chill of the house seeking his flesh made him shiver. He wrapped the robe tighter. In his own home, surrounded by familiar things, encased within memorized walls, his wife within the sound of his voice, yet he felt alone.

He thought of Bertrand. Not just alone, but isolated, in a cell. His only contact would be with strangers, unfamiliar beings who thought him to be the most repulsive of humans...a killer.

If he were guilty then it is the consequence of his actions, rational or not, his own. If innocent then... fear...confusion...desperation...panic. If innocent, Bertrand's only hope was the truth. Not much consolation. Both Gambrelli and Bertrand knew that the truth did not always appear when needed.

He returned to the phone.

"Police Headquarters," he said to the operator.

Drumming his fingers on the console he waited.

"Metropolitan Police," the switchboard operator said.

"The duty sergeant, please." He set the receiver down and crossed the room to retrieve his coffee cup, hurrying back to the phone just in time.

"Sergeant Duran," the lethargic voice droned.

"Good morning, Duran: this is Gambrelli."

"Chief Inspector didn't you and your men just leave here?"

"I want you to take a message for Detective Sergeant Andres, and make sure he gets it as soon as he comes in."

"Fire away."

"Tell him I had to leave town. He's going to have to handle the Marcus hearing this morning. I won't be able to call him until later in the day." Gambrelli stretched the phone cord toward the table trying to reach the ashtray.

"Got it. Where you heading?"

"To the coast, on the six o'clock train."

"I'll send a car around to pick you up."

"Don't waste a man on that, I'll take a taxi."

"It's no waste. I've got an officer here with a car waiting to be summoned by Superintendent Wilhelm,"

"What's Wilhelm got going?"

"Absolutely nothing, as usual. He just wants an officer and a car standing by twenty-four hours a day, in case he needs one." Duran's voice lowered. "Damn shame to waste a patrolman on every shift for that imperial bag of wind."

"When did this start?" Gambrelli reached again toward the ashtray. The tension on the receiver cord pulled the base of the phone precariously close to the edge of the cabinet.

"First of the month. It was in a department memorandum."

"Signed by the commissioner?" Gambrelli gave up on the ashtray and rubbed the back of his hand against his unshaven chin.

"Wilhelm signed it himself. Commissioner DeMartell would never sign off on something like that. The Commissioner still walks to headquarters every morning, rain or shine." The sentence was followed by the sound of Sergeant Duran lighting one of his stubby cigars and puffing it to life. "I'll have the officer in front of your place in thirty minutes, and don't refuse. It will do the lad good to drive a real policeman for a change."

Gambrelli returned to the table, lit a cigarette and slurped his coffee, licking the rim before setting the half empty cup on the saucer. He heard Odin rumbling down the stairs. A moment later the dog's square head was resting on the table top an inch from the cup and saucer.

"No croissant this morning, my friend."

Odin shifted his weight and nudged closer to the cup.

"Life is a funny thing ..." He rubbed the dog's head. "One never knows when it is lifting you up just to hurl you against the rocks."

The dog snorted and walked back upstairs.

"You're right, it doesn't matter. Bertrand's guilt or innocence will be determined by the evidence. The facts will speak for themselves."

Alone again in the dim light Gambrelli ran his hand along the dark wood of the table top. It had taken him years to find this table. It was almost identical to the one in the kitchen of his boyhood home. In his memory that massive table of his youth had been the center of his family life.

Ten years ago, upon his father's death, the ancestral home and the surrounding vineyards had passed to Gambrelli, the eldest child and only son.

He leaned forward and picked up the cup. *Ten years ago*, he thought. Had it been that long?

At the time he had been so immersed in his work he had never entertained the thought of retiring and returning to the village to run the family business. His sister, her husband, and three children were already living in the small guest house on the family property. So it had seemed sensible to encourage them to move into the main house and continue their work with the vineyards.

All Gambrelli really wanted was the kitchen table. Instead he gave the table, the house, and half the business to his sister. It was the only sensible thing to do.

Once he realized the family table would never be his, he spent a year rummaging through second hand shops and antique stores in search of a suitable replacement. His efforts resulted in this table, this substitute. He rubbed the edge of the thick wood as an apology for thinking of it as merely a replacement. But that is what it was.

Not that there was anything wrong with this table. It was finely constructed of sturdy walnut, pegged with oak, darkened and smoothed by years of wear. He was glad to have it.

But it would never be the table he coveted.

Not the one on which he had learned to write. Not the one at which he had sat at his father's side and listened to stories of his ancestors and the planting of the first vines. Not the table that held the meal during which he announced his engagement to Marie. Not the table around which the Gambrelli family celebrated the births of his son and two daughters.

When his mother died he had seen his father's tears fall onto that table, not this table. He remembered sitting silently as his father wiped the tears from the worn wood with the edge of his calloused hand and said, "My only friend is gone. I shall miss her more than I can ever say." To the best of Gambrelli's recollection his father never mentioned his mother again.

•   •   •

Marie stood in the bathroom doorway watching her husband shave. Over her shoulder he could see that Odin had climbed onto the bed and was comfortably resting his head on Gambrelli's pillow.

"Don't forget to take that razor, and pack your bathing suit and some light clothing," she said.

"Don't be ridiculous, I'm not going on holiday." He wiped his face with a damp towel. "And it's too cold for summer suits."

"It may be chilly here, but that far south it's still hot. I read it in the paper yesterday, 'unseasonably warm,' they said." She took the towel from his hand and folded it over the porcelain bar next to the bath.

"You will scare the natives and the tourists if you lumber around that resort island in your black wool suit and overcoat. They will think a great gray-headed bear has come to ravage them."

"Be grateful I don't ravage you."

"You haven't the time." She kissed him and went back to bed.

THE ISLAND OF Q

FOUR

Unseasonably warm," Gambrelli muttered as he stepped from the gangway of the ferry onto the dock.

The heat was oppressive. The sun pushed heavily on the shoulders of his starched, white shirt. Gambrelli had been to the island on several occasions, but did not remember September being quite this hot.

Sweat soaked his collar and ran against his ribs. Even with the vast expanse of water on either side of the narrow dock there was not the slightest breath of air to cool him. Fishing boats in need of fresh paint lined the dock, swaying listlessly with the exhausted tide.

He pushed against the heat toward a café at the end of the long dock. Half way there he set down his valise. He had packed in the dark, two hours before dawn. Had he remembered his razor? He dropped his suit coat on the leather handle of the case and dried his hands against his black trousers. He loosened his tie, rolled up his sleeves, picked up the valise and moved slowly toward the café.

He wished he had followed Marie's advice and lost some weight. Maybe then the heat would not seem so bad. "I'm too old for exercise," he had told her.

"Fifty-four is not old my dear. The best years are ahead," she'd said.

He shrugged and continued reading the paper. He had wanted to say, "Let me die in peace." Instead he agreed that when the cool weather returned he would begin a fitness regimen of calisthenics he had learned in the army. Satisfied with her victory she had kissed him on the top of his head and returned to the kitchen humming a tune he could not identify.

Small trees along the café's veranda and a faded blue awning provided some shade. He dropped into a wooden chair next to a marble table. Above his head pale blue letters on a white background identified the café as the Island Tavern. The trees and the awning gave no perceptible relief from the heat. From inside, he heard the shuffling of sandals moving slowly on a sandy, wooden floor.

Gambrelli looked at his own shoes—heavy soles, black leather, better suited to stepping on necks than navigating the crushed shells and sand of the seaside town. A small crab with only one claw crawled sideways from under the table, poking at the edge of his shoe. He kicked the invalid crab to the side, immediately regretting the effort as sweat ran down his calf into his sock.

"Something to drink?" The proprietor called from the doorway, apparently unwilling to step out onto the hot patio if the answer was to be "No."

"Some water, with lemon," he said.

The proprietor's corpulent, red face sagged. He exhaled a breath of disgust. Gambrelli sympathized with the unspoken message in the proprietor's sigh: *All the way across the café, an arduous journey that must be repeated, all for a glass of water. What else could be expected from a stranger, dressed like a lunatic banker?*

"And a glass of cold white wine," Gambrelli added, to ease the proprietor's burden.

He didn't want the wine. Several glasses on the train from the city to the coast, and another on the ferry to the island had dulled his senses, and as his wife always said, made the heat more oppressive.

He finished the wine and ordered another. The proprietor's sandals approached with the second glass at a quickened pace.

"Are you here about the murdered woman?" The proprietor tried to hand him the glass. Gambrelli did not move. The proprietor set the glass on the table. "I heard someone was coming from the City."

"What else have you heard?" Gambrelli saw the crab move cautiously toward his black shoe.

"Nothing that wasn't in the newspaper. My morning customers come and go before the rag hits the street. All they talked of was the heat driving the fish deeper. And that a storm is to blow in tonight and cool things off."

"Bring me the paper."

Gambrelli watched the crab slowly approach and poke the shoe leather tentatively, as if expecting another kick.

"Curiosity, tenacity, and a degree of caution," he said to the crab, "Admirable qualities, little one. Most admirable."

The proprietor returned and laid the newspaper next to the glass.

"I will know more when the regulars come in tonight. By then they'll have all the gossip from their wives and the hags at the town market." The proprietor lingered as if expecting more conversation. None was offered. He shuffled back into the dark of the café.

Near the end of the second glass a police vehicle stopped in front of the café. A thin and darkly tanned young man, dressed in the uniform of a sergeant in the Provincial Police, stepped from the car.

"Chief Inspector Gambrelli?" the sergeant asked, as a matter of form.

"Quite a lucky guess," Gambrelli mumbled to himself. Who else would be dressed so inappropriately for the heat, other than a Metropolitan Police Inspector, thee hundred kilometers south of his jurisdictional boundaries?

"Major Ormond is tied up in a meeting with the mayor, he asked me to pick you up and take you to Headquarters."

"Take me to the Parc Hotel." He tucked the newspaper under his arm, slipped the cost of the wine, and a generous tip, under the glass.

He tossed his valise and black suit coat in the back seat of the car. He settled himself against the hot upholstery as they drove along the sandy road into the middle of town. Looking straight ahead Gambrelli listened without comment as the sergeant, assuming the role of tour guide, pointed out buildings of historical significance.

A doorman, in khaki shirt and trousers, showed no interest as the police car pulled under the portico of the hotel entrance. He waited until the passenger opened the rear door and pulled out a bag and coat before slowly approaching the car and extending a thin arm of assistance.

Gambrelli ignored the doorman's effort to take hold of the black valise. Pushing the car door closed with his foot he said through the open window, "Tell Ormond I will be in his office within the hour."

He turned toward the hotel entrance as the doorman's hand clamped firmly on the handle of the valise. Gambrelli did not let go.

"Is it the suitcase or the tip you're trying to hold on to?" The doorman tugged harder.

A grin spread across Gambrelli's face as he released the bag.

"Do you always speak to the guests this way?"

"Only the ones that are delivered by the police."
The doorman motioned for Gambrelli to proceed.
"Do the police bring many clients to the hotel?"
"No, you're the first."

FIVE

The Parc Hotel was several steps above his expectations. The lobby, decorated with oriental carpets and dwarf palms in polished brass pots, was adjoined on one end by a well-appointed bar and on the other by a dining room formalized with white tablecloths and gleaming stemware. The desk clerk, accustomed to dealing with tourists, requested Gambrelli's passport prior to handing over the room key.

"That won't be necessary," Gambrelli said.

"It is a police requirement, Monsieur Gambrelli," the clerk asserted in his most officious tone, holding the room key close to his chest.

Gambrelli pulled his Metropolitan Police identity card from his coat and stuck it under the clerk's nose.

"Of course, Chief Inspector, your passport won't be necessary." The clerk replaced the key on a rack behind the desk and chose another. "I think you will find this room more to your liking." He handed over the new key. "The elevator is across the lobby to your right."

Gambrelli glanced in the direction of the elevator. He looked at the key. The fob read *206*. "The stairs?" he asked.

"Past the elevator on the other side of the bar."

The hotel room was larger than Gambrelli expected. The shuttered windows and thick plaster walls repelled the heat from the street. He placed a hand against the pale green wall and found it to be pleasantly cool. Above the bed, the large rattan blades of a ceiling fan moved the air just enough to dry the moisture in his clothing.

Gambrelli unpacked the valise and was pleased to find his razor. He took a washcloth from a stack of towels in the armoire, ran it under the faucet, and placed it at the back of his neck.

He spread the newspaper on a table near the shuttered window and read the article that took up only half a column on the front page.

> *Provincial Police reported the discovery of the body of local shop owner Annette Cuomo in her home last night, shortly after eleven.*
>
> *Initial reports indicated Cuomo was the victim of a homicide.*
>
> *Neighbors of the victim said they neither heard nor saw anything out of the ordinary Tuesday evening that would have indicated*

a problem at Cuomo's cottage located along Beach Road.

Major Henri Ormond said the police have a suspect in custody but refused to provide any additional information. It is reported by a source close to the investigation that the suspect is a tourist residing at the Parc Hotel and had arrived on the Island earlier in the day.

Gambrelli took his notebook from the valise and added the name Annette Cuomo, and the fact that she owned a shop, to the notes he had made when Commissioner DeMartell called in the middle of the night.

He started to prepare to leave then sat down. He was agitated. The sergeant's words, 'Major Ormond is tied up in a meeting with the mayor...' repeated inside his head. Over the years he had encountered many police officers, and commanders, assigned to small towns who conducted themselves as if they were the personal servants of the local politicians. It was, Gambrelli had rationalized, natural for a local police commander, who relished his position, to refrain from antagonizing those who could terminate his employment. Ormond, however, was a major in the Provincial Police. He reported to the superintendent in Paris. It was very unlikely that a mayor, on a coastal island, would be able to exert any influence on the major's career.

"Perhaps the major is just a congenial fellow, meeting on matters unrelated to the case at hand," Gambrelli said aloud as he pulled the damp cloth from his neck.

He imagined Bertrand waiting for his arrival. Even if Gambrelli was not a friendly face at least he would be a familiar one...a morning breeze that carried the scent of home.

SIX

The interior walls of the Provincial Police Head-quarters were a darker shade of green than the pastel green of his hotel room. Major Henri Ormond stood ramrod straight behind an over-sized desk. His thin moustache curved upward at the ends, accentuating his gaunt face, and lending a quality of the Foreign Legion to his stiffly pressed khaki uniform. After a flurry of standard professional pleasantries, Ormond related the details of the investigation to Gambrelli.

"The call came in last night at eleven-fifteen. The caller, Joseph Krantz, claims to be the victim's friend. He is a local artist, watercolors and post-cards mostly. He discovered the body."

"Where is Krantz now?"

"We have him in custody, but will probably release him shortly."

"I'd like to talk to him before he is released."

"Of course," Ormond's tone indicated that Gambrelli's request had been anticipated. "When my men arrived, Krantz was standing outside the cottage. The body of Annette Cuomo was found on the bed. Her hands were tied behind her back. She—"

"Tied with what?"

"A red and yellow man's tie. Silk." Ormond referred to the report. "Her throat was slashed and there were several superficial wounds on her chest and abdomen. There were bruises on her shoulders, her wrists, and one on her right cheek."

"The weapon?"

"A large kitchen knife was found on the floor of the bedroom."

"Blood on the blade?" Gambrelli kept his remarks brief in response to the clipped tone set by the Major.

"It had been wiped clean, but some near the handle."

"Fingerprints?" Gambrelli pulled his notebook from his jacket.

"Three on the handle. They are only partial prints, but the preliminary examination has identified them as belonging to Bertrand." Ormond closed the file on his desk and looked at Gambrelli who ignored the Major's apparent attitude that the case was all but concluded.

"Why wipe the knife blade and not the handle. And why leave the weapon at the scene?" Gambrelli shifted in his chair.

"Who can say what compels a murderer." Ormond dismissed the thought with a shrug. "Krantz told the officers that the victim was meeting with Jean Michel Bertrand to advise him that she no longer wanted to see him."

"How did he know this?"

"She told him."

"Just like that? 'I am kicking my lover down the road this evening,' Why would she—"

"Apparently they are very good friends...she had confided in him earlier in the day."

"What was Krantz doing at the victim's home after eleven?"

"They were to meet at Krantz' studio at ten. When she did not arrive by ten-forty-five he went to look for her."

"And if Krantz was more than just a friend, maybe a hopeful suitor, and upon arrival found that Annette had changed her mind and decided to remain with Bertrand...."

"That's why we took him into custody. However, when we located Bertrand at his hotel room, my officers found a white shirt, monogrammed with Bertrand's initials, stuffed in the cupboard under his bathroom sink. The shirt was smeared with blood."

"The victim's blood?"

"Yes."

"What did Bertrand say about that?"

"At the time, nothing, he was too drunk to know what was going on. In his statement today he claims he had left the shirt at the victim's home."

"And the red and yellow tie?"

"Bertrand admitted it is his. And that he left it at Mademoiselle Cuomo's home as well." Major Ormond leaned forward. "Under my interrogation, Bertrand also admitted bringing the knife to her home last night. It was one of a set of three; the other two were still in the gift box on the kitchen table."

"Did Bertrand confess a motive for the crime?" Gambrelli asked.

"He denies any knowledge of the murder. He did say they had an argument."

"Bertrand admitted that?"

"Yes and that Cuomo was leaving him for a younger man," Ormond said, as if offering the perfect explanation for murder. He raised his right eyebrow and seemed to be waiting for the Chief Inspector's acknowledgement.

Gambrelli did not react, other than to jot additional notes. He continued to listen with wavering interest in Ormond's conjectures. The Major kept talking, but Gambrelli was already thinking of Bertrand.

"After I talk to Bertrand, I would like to see the murder scene and the hotel room," Gambrelli said.

"Both locations have been secured. My men are posted and have instructions to provide you with every courtesy." Ormond pushed the file to the corner of the desk. "I have met with the mayor and we would like you to know that you are to consider yourself our guest. Whatever we can do to make your stay more pleasant will be done. And it is expected that you will provide me with any insight into this case that may occur to you."

"Thank you." Gambrelli started to rise.

"I must emphasize the operative word 'guest.'" Ormond paused, apparently struggling to find the right words.

Gambrelli focused intently on the Major's eyes, trying to discern the reason for his sudden hesitance.

"You are out of your jurisdiction, Chief Inspector," Ormond said, a slight flush rising across his face. "You are not authorized to act unilaterally while you are here. Your authority is strictly limited to that of observer."

Gambrelli ignored Ormond's needless assertion of authority. He felt embarrassed for Ormond being required to parrot a warning obviously concocted by the mayor.

He returned the notebook to his jacket pocket.

"The newspaper said the victim was a local shop owner. Can I assume your men have that location secured?" Gambrelli asked.

"I will put a man on it." Ormond's response was authoritative.

Gambrelli recognized the tone as one often employed by his supervisor, Superintendent Wilhelm, to compensate for the embarrassment of an obvious oversight.

"I'd like to speak to Jean Michel Bertrand now."

SEVEN

Without the benefit of a ceiling fan, or window, the small interview room was stifling. Bertrand emitted the scent of musk tinged with the sour smell of drunkard's vomit. Missing was the acrid smell of urine, drying on damp trousers, for which Gambrelli was grateful. He forced himself to meet Bertrand's eyes without betraying his discomfort at seeing the prosecutor in this condition.

On the small wooden table between them was a tin plate marred with the soot of extinguished cigarettes. Gambrelli took a pack from his coat and offered one to Bertrand. The prosecutor's hand was listless as he reached for it. Gambrelli, eager to fill his mouth and nose with smoke, lit his own before sliding his lighter across the table.

The prosecutor inhaled deeply. He attempted to pull the collar of his shirt higher on his neck and smooth its rumpled front. Gambrelli watched the long pale fingers press against the beige seashell design. The loose-fitting, flimsy garment made the prosecutor appear even more tragic than his circumstance. Gambrelli had not worn such a shirt since he was a youth. Even when on vacation, or working in his family vineyard during the harvest, he preferred a white shirt with a black vest. Gambrelli's only concession to the atmosphere of leisure was confined to turning his sleeves a fold or two along his thick forearms. Short sleeves, like the prosecutor was wearing, would never cross his mind. He was not a school boy.

He waited for Bertrand to gather his composure. When he had first entered the tiny room Bertrand had jumped to his feet and greeted him with relief. "Arthur, thank God you're here."

Gambrelli had known Bertrand for twenty years and in all that time he could not remember the prosecutor ever calling him by his Christian name. When they were being civil to each other Bertrand had always called him by his title, first it was sergeant, then detective, later inspector, and for the last ten years, chief inspector. When they were at odds the Prosecutor usually prefaced his statements with, "Damn you, Gambrelli." Being called "Arthur" derailed him a bit, so he had responded, "Monsieur Prosecutor," to set the train right.

"Chief Inspector, I know we have not always seen eye to eye. And at times I have been critical of your methods, but...."

Gambrelli flicked an ash onto the tin plate and used the cigarette to wave off any further discussion of their past encounters.

"When and how did you meet the…" Gambrelli caught himself before using the term victim, "…did you meet Mademoiselle Annette Cuomo?"

"Two years ago, in the City. My wife Adele had purchased a painting at the Savage Gallery. She asked me to stop by and approve the purchase before shipment. Normally she would not even have sought my approval, but the painting was very expensive, even by Adele's standard. Annette was working there as a sales girl."

Gambrelli knew the gallery; it had been part of his patrol beat when he was a new officer. The original owner was a banker who purchased the gallery for his wife as an amusement. A year later she ran off with a Spanish painter. Gambrelli wondered how many love affairs began and ended with the Savage Gallery.

"Soon I became a regular at the gallery, always timing my visits to coincide with Annette's presence. We would talk, she made me laugh."

Bertrand continued, providing exacting details of his blossoming relationship with Annette. Gambrelli thought of interrupting. He had no interest in useless information. He had his own questions to be answered, but the recollection of the past seemed to give Bertrand a new energy. Gambrelli suffered the narration, hoping it would make the prosecutor's memory more precise.

There was nothing new in Bertrand's story. Gambrelli had heard it dozens of times, usually as part of a suspect's confession. To outsiders the Bertrands had the perfect life. Both were from families of prominence. They had wealth, social position, a very comfortable, if not extravagant, lifestyle with servants and an elegant residence. *If only they were not human*, Gambrelli thought. The basic human need to be loved and to love in return was their downfall. As it was the downfall of many, regardless of economic position.

Succumbing to the heat, Gambrelli drifted on the edge of sleep as Bertrand gave a rambling account of the deterioration of his marriage to Adele. In typical fashion, it all started off so wonderfully. A young couple in love, with hopes and dreams turn into strangers, each intolerant or indifferent to the other. The soft and passionate kisses become brisk pecks on the cheek, grudgingly given by wooden lips. Embraces are reduced to a pat on the arm so as not to be perceived as requesting intimacy, a request that experience had taught him would undoubtedly be rejected. She no longer listens to his stories of victory or minor setback, but dismisses his concerns, preferring instead to tell him of her frustration with the butcher or the details of a new tapestry for the hall.

Finally, they grow weary of the charade. He immerses himself in his work and ignores his life at home. She occupies herself with the children, friends, or charities, and never admits that she no longer feels like a woman. And so they go, often for years, or to the grave, sacrificing their dreams for reasons they never comprehend.

Occasionally, as in Prosecutor Bertrand's case, there is an unexpected interruption to the surrender. He met, quite by accident, a charming face. It happens to men. She may be younger, or older, but generally younger. She looks at him with fresh eyes. She is interested in every aspect of his life. They laugh together. He hasn't really laughed in years. They have a meaningless cup of coffee, share a pastry, then lunch, a drink after work, and soon a romantic dinner. He has no one to answer to. His wife has long ago accepted his physical and emotional absence.

"Annette made me realize how empty my life had become. How I had abandoned my dreams and resolved myself to believing death was the only solution to my loneliness." Bertrand looked at Gambrelli as if requesting some indication of understanding and compassion.

Gambrelli stared at him with indifference. He wanted to say: "What do you want from me? I am not a priest to give absolution, or your wife to grant forgiveness. You are a man, obligated to your commitments. Honor them and stop whining like a spoiled child." Instead, as an inducement to continue, he nodded, but Bertrand seemed to have read his face and fell silent.

"How did you choose this island? There are many discreet locations closer to the City." Gambrelli asked to ease the prisoner back into conversation.

"It was Annette who talked of it. At first as a dream, an imagined life together, and then one day I decided why not. We came here together and found the gallery for lease, and the cottage. I put deposits on both."

"Your wife did not suspect?

"No. I have several investment properties in the City and in the countryside." Bertrand gained an air of propriety. "Adele's only concern was that the investment should turn a profit. I insisted that she come here to see for herself."

"Did she?"

"Yes."

"You did not think it a risk to show her the exact location of your love nest?" Gambrelli tried not to make it sound like an accusation, but another description evaded him.

"Adele hates the beach, the sand annoys her. The casual atmosphere insults her sense of dignity. The day we were here we had lunch near the shop. I was extra fortunate: her meal was mediocre, the service terrible, a vacationing family at the next table lost control of their children, and the parents erupted in a loud dispute. All together that was enough to en-sure Adele would never return here for any reason."

Gambrelli couldn't suppress a smile at the thought of Adele Bertrand being forced to endure contact with the travails of ordinary life. "How often do you come here, to be with Annette?"

"Once a week … usually just for the day, sometimes two. I catch the early train from the Central Station and arrive here by late morning. The last ferry to the mainland leaves every night at six and the last train to the city arrives at the Central Station shortly after ten. I'm home before eleven."

"Your wife doesn't require an explanation?" Gambrelli wrote the time schedule in his notebook.

"I come here on Tuesdays, just like yesterday. Tuesday night Adele always goes to the theater, or a concert, with her friends, followed by a light dinner. She is rarely home before midnight."

"Does she go out with the same friends every week?"

"Mostly the same."

"Their names?" Gambrelli wrote the names. One in particular, Julienne Vercel, was familiar to him. "And on the occasions when you stay on the island for two days, how do you explain that?"

"I told Adele as senior prosecutor I was required to consult periodically with the provincial authorities on criminal matters. She takes no interest in my work, so she has no perspective on how absurd that story is." Bertrand took another cigarette from the pack on the table. "She actually thought it fortunate that the ministry would provide travel and lodging expenses for me to check on our investment here."

"How long has this been going on?"

"About six months."

"What time did you arrive yesterday?"

"Not until after six, I was delayed at the office."

"Did you go straight from the ferry to Annette's?"

"No. When I spend the night I always check into the Parc Hotel, in case Adele calls for me. The desk clerk holds all my messages." He exhaled a cloud of smoke in Gambrelli's direction.

"So what time did you get to the cottage?"

"Just before sunset, about eight I guess. I brought a bottle of champagne."

"What brand?"

"Laurent-Perrier, twenty-seven."

"An auspicious year. Where did you buy it?"

"At the hotel."

"Was that usual?"

"No, it was a celebration bottle. I was going to tell Annette that I had decided to leave Adele, resign my position and move to the island." The Prosecutor's eyes welled with tears.

Despite his detachment Gambrelli's thoughts were halted by this revelation.

"I had also brought Annette a gift, a box of kitchen knives."

Having lost his investigative footing he asked the first inane question that came to mind. "Did you buy the knives locally?"

"No they're from Valencin's...on rue Pizey... near Palaise des Artes."

"How many knives were in the box?" Gambrelli stayed on the subject looking for an indication that Bertrand knew a knife from that box was the murder weapon.

"Three, a large chef's knife, a utility knife and a paring knife."

Bertrand was undisturbed. He was either a psychopath, or had not been informed as to the weapon of death.

Gambrelli felt the blood rush to his face. He had not asked Ormond what details Bertrand had been told. It was a foolish, incompetent oversight. Bertrand was calmly waiting for him to continue, so he assumed for the moment the prosecutor was ignorant and sane.

"What did you do upon arrival at the cottage?"

"I changed clothes as was my custom. I keep a small wardrobe there so I can shed the constraints of my formal attire. Annette has bought me several of these resort shirts to wear." He smoothed the front of the shirt again.

"And the clothes you removed, what did you do with them?"

"I only changed my shirt as I was anxious to tell Annette the news of my decision." He thought for a moment. "I left my dress shirt and tie on the bed. My suit coat, I hung by the kitchen door."

"Did you argue?"

"No, it wasn't an argument. She told me she had fallen in love with another man. A younger man."

"And this did not anger you?"

Bertrand looked down at the end of his cigarette. "What is a man to do? A reasonable man.
What is there to do, but walk away."

"Did she tell you his name? Where he lived? His
line of work?"

"No.

"Did you strike her?"

"No," Bertrand responded as if insulted. "All I
ever wanted was for her to be happy. I knew the risk
of leaving her alone for such long periods of time.
Nights and days alone for any woman are difficult.
For Annette it was especially hard, she is so loving,
so full of life and affection that I feared this outcome from the start."

"What time did you leave the cottage?"

"After nine. I got back to the hotel at nine-thirty."

"And did you take your shirt, tie, and jacket
with you when you left?"

"The jacket only. I almost went back to get the
shirt and tie, but decided not to. I didn't want to go
back."

Gradually Bertrand related the rest of the evening with Gambrelli's questioning to guide him and
elicit every remembered detail. He had arrived at
the hotel, avoided contact with anyone, carrying his
jacket. He couldn't stay in his room, it was too hot.
He went to the bar and drank brandy. He eventually decided to return to the cottage, but halfway
there, too drunk to navigate the path, he fell. The
fall sobered him enough to return to his room.

No, Bertrand did not think anyone saw him.
If they did he did not notice. The heat in the hotel
room made him dizzy. He cried, became ill, vom-
ited several times and finally threw himself on the
bed and passed out. His next recollection was of
police officers standing over him, ordering him not
to move. They arrested him, threw him in a cell and
questioned him about his activities. In the end they
told him Annette had been murdered.

"Have you had mistresses before Annette?"

"No."

"Why this one?"

"I have no idea. It just happened. I never
planned it."

"Was Adele suspicious?"

"No. She never said anything."

"Did you ever discuss with anyone your intention to leave your wife?"

"Only in the vaguest terms, a few weeks ago; I
had lunch with Charles Goddard. You know him?"

"Everyone knows he has made a fortune repre-
senting parties in high profile divorces." Gambrelli
made more notes. "Could anyone have seen you
together?"

"We met at the University Club. Goddard and I
were classmates at university, lunch together could
be explained."

"Your wife never goes to the club?"

"Women are only allowed on Saturday eve-
nings. We were there a few weeks ago for a charity

dinner Adele had organized to benefit the new wing of the Hôtel Dieu."

"Was it before, or after, your luncheon with Goddard?"

"The following evening, I believe. The exact dates will be in my appointment book at my office."

"And no one could have told your wife of your luncheon with the divorce attorney Goddard?" Gambrelli continued to make notes without looking at Bertrand.

"I can't imagine who—"

"After this Saturday night at the club, did your wife act in any way out of character, or differently toward you?"

"No, not especially. Although, she did suggest we might take a few days away, at the Chalet Vignoble in the hill country."

"And what was your response?"

"I said we might. We had been there several times in the first few years of our marriage. Actually it was the thought of being away with my wife and unable to see Annette that convinced me, beyond all doubt, that my devotion was to Annette."

"After she moved to the island, did Annette ever return to the City?"

"No...well once, last week."

"When was the last time you and Annette were together in the City?"

"Last Tuesday. She told me not to come to the island that day because she was coming to the City to see her younger sister, Lisa, about some family problem. She arrived on the last train. I surprised her by meeting her train at the station...she had told me not to bother. We walked to a nearby café for a bite; she was too agitated to eat. She left me before our meal was served. She just stood up and said, 'I must go.' I was so taken by surprise I just sat there and watched her rush out the door."

"Agitated about what, did she say?"

"No."

"Where does her sister live?"

"The last I knew she was in the University District, on Leopold Street, a block north of the Textile Museum. A second floor apartment, I don't recall the street number."

"How well do you know the sister Lisa?"

"Not very well."

"But you have spent time with her?"

"A little, she has been to dinner with us on a few occasions." Bertrand gave a questioning look.

"Have you ever spent time alone with her?"

"Gambrelli, I can't see where this line of questioning—"

"Answer the question." Gambrelli asserted his position as interrogator. "Time alone, just the two of you."

"Only when the sisters shared an apartment in the City, sometimes I would arrive early and wait for Annette to get home from work," Bertrand paused then added, "And a few times in the last six months we had lunch, Lisa and I, near the Ministry."

"And this would have been after Annette moved here and opened her shop?"

"Yes."

"Were these luncheons at your invitation or hers?"

"By accident actually; at Chez Charles...near the Palais de Justice. I'm sure you know it. I ran into her on the street, so I offered to take her for a meal and she accepted. The other times it was the same."

"Always at Chez Charles?" Gambrelli knew the restaurant. It was what he would call an intimate café, set off the street in a narrow passageway, the food a step above the local bouchons with prices to match. It was considered more Parisian than regional which kept it in perpetual disfavor among the locals.

"Yes."

"Her choice or yours?"

Bertrand was slow to reply. "She suggested it... said it was her favorite—"

"During these luncheons were you observed by anyone you knew?"

"I don't recall... probably not. What would it matter?"

"Did she say what she was she doing in the area of the Palais de Justice?"

"She was processing through a series of interviews for a position with Cramer Brokerage. Their offices are located along the river, north of the Ministry building."

Gambrelli scratched his pen on the pad. The ink had stopped flowing. He shook the pen, sending a galaxy of tiny pools of ink across the page. The pen repaired, he continued to write.

"How would you characterize the relationship between Annette and Lisa?"

"Like that of any siblings; loving, occasionally contentious."

"Did they argue?"

"Not in front of me, but at times I could tell the relationship was a bit strained." Bertrand lit another cigarette. "They were so different. I guess a degree of friction was to be expected."

"Different in what way?"

"Lisa is a few years younger, impulsive, caught up in the modern life, the latest fashion, the popular scene. You know how young people are these days."

"Annette was not old," Gambrelli took a handkerchief from his pocket and wiped his brow.

"No, but she was more mature, intellectual, concerned with the seriousness of life."

"Did Annette have any other relatives?"

"Not that she ever mentioned, just her sister."

"Their parents, where are they?"

"Both dead. The father died several years ago. The mother about eight months ago ... after a long painful illness. Following the mother's death, Lisa moved to the City to live with Annette." Bertrand paused, and pulled the ashtray closer to his side of the table then continued. "I was just thinking... about their arguments... It may have been that with the parents dead Annette assumed the role of Lisa's protector... unconsciously allowing her maternal instincts to take over. I cautioned her about being too protective, but she said she couldn't help it."

"Getting back to last Tuesday, Annette left you at the restaurant. Did you meet with her the following day?" Gambrelli held the pen close to his nose and examined the gold nib.

"We were supposed to meet at a pastry shop near the Savage Gallery. She never showed up."

Gambrelli waited.

"I was walking to the Gallery when I saw my wife get out of a cab and go in. I watched from a book shop across the street. A few minutes later she came out, following a man. She stopped him near the corner and they spoke briefly before getting into a cab together. I looked in the gallery windows. Annette was not there, so I returned to my office."

"Who was the man?"

"I have no idea."

"Describe him."

"Tall, my height, dark hair, early-forties, well dressed, I only saw him for a moment. I never asked my wife about it—how could I?—and she never mentioned it."

"And the next time you saw Annette?"

"Last night."

Gambrelli made more notes. He wiped the handkerchief across the back of his neck and under his chin.

"Did she ever tell you about her former lovers?" Gambrelli asked.

"Once, she started to tell me of a man. He was an importer of fresh produce. She went to work for him as a bookkeeper soon after she moved to the City. He was kind to her at first, and paid her an exorbitant wage, the bulk of which she sent to help support her mother and sister. Soon it became apparent that her employer expected more than her accounting skills in return for his generosity. A relationship developed between them, but he became abusive and violent. She told me she was afraid of him, but when I pressed her for details she refused to discuss it."

"Did she give this man a name?"

"Philippe. She only spoke it once, and then implored me to take her away, far away, from the City."

"Did she tell you the name of his company?"

"No, but I believe it is somewhere in the City's Harbor District. I once tried to take her to a restaurant in that area, and when we pulled in front to park, she would not get out of the car. She'd said it held too many horrible memories for her."

"Do you recall the name of the restaurant?"

"The Brigand, it's a few blocks—"

"I know it." Gambrelli closed his notebook. "You said Annette's mother died after a long illness?"

"Yes."

"And during that illness was Lisa her only caretaker?"

"Yes, as far as I know."

Gambrelli put the notepad in his coat and stood up.

"Where are you going?" Bertrand asked.

"To make some inquiries." Gambrelli hesitated. "Who other than you and Lisa knew Annette was living on this island?"

"No one that I am aware of, I never told anyone."

"And the sister, Lisa, would she have said something?"

"What reason would she have to say anything?" Bertrand asked.

"I was hoping you could tell me."

"Chief Inspector, I am not responsible for Annette's death."

Gambrelli placed his hands on the table and leaned toward the prosecutor.

"You met a young woman, seduced her into becoming your mistress then moved her from her home to this island where she has been murdered." Gambrelli stepped back from the table. "You may not be the killer, but you are not without some degree of responsibility."

Gambrelli walked out of the interview room, leaving the pack of cigarettes on the table.

EIGHT

The officer assigned to secure Annette Cuomo's cottage was sitting at the kitchen table smoking and drinking a cup of tea. He snapped to attention as Gambrelli entered and displayed his identity card as a matter of form.

"Chief Inspector, I've been waiting for you," the officer said, not looking at the offered identification.

Gambrelli nodded and walked past him. After twenty minutes alone in the bedroom and living room, Gambrelli returned to the kitchen and addressed the officer. "I did not see a telephone."

"There's no phone service on this side of Beach Road."

Gambrelli checked his notes.

"So from where did this Joseph Krantz call the police?"

"From the Auberge de Phare. It is on the other side of the road about a half kilometer to the right from the end of the path."

"And the proprietor of the inn has been questioned and confirms the events as told by Krantz?"

"Yes."

"Do you have a list of items removed from the house?"

The officer produced a sheet of paper from his shirt pocket.

Gambrelli examined it. "There was a bottle of champagne on the table. It is not on the list," Gambrelli said.

"I don't know—"

"And I noticed there were no keys in the house. I would assume the victim had at least two keys, one for this cottage and one for her store. Yet there are none listed on this inventory. So where did they go?"

"I was not—"

"Call your headquarters and see if the bottle and keys were removed."

"If they had been taken, they would be on the list. It is procedure."

"Sometimes there is an oversight." Gambrelli softened his tone. "Please double-check."

He was standing in the bedroom when the officer returned. "No, Chief Inspector, there was no bottle of champagne nor any key or keys removed from the house."

"And was there a search made of this room?"

"Not yet. The victim's body was taken to the coroner's office at the hospital, and the items on the

inventory list were removed at Major Ormond's instruction. But no search of the premises was made."

"Look here." Gambrelli opened the drawers of
an oak dresser, and then led the officer to the closet.
"Does it not appear that a search of these areas has
taken place?"

"If there has been a search, I can assure you it
was not by the provincial police. I have been posted
here since the removal of the body. No one has been
in or out until you arrived."

"You see the pry marks on the closet floor and
the loosened boards? There at the edges, where the
floor boards meet the interior wall of the closet."
Gambrelli stepped back to allow the officer to kneel
down and run his hand along the boards. "Have
you seen a tool capable of making such marks anywhere in the house?"

"No, but there is a shed attached to the side of
the cottage. I will check."

A few minutes later, the policeman returned
without a tool to match the pry marks. Gambrelli
was not surprised. A killer who would throw the
murder weapon on the bedroom floor was certainly
not likely to replace a tool. *But why not leave the
tool on the floor as well?*

"Perhaps one will be discovered in the tall grass
outside, or along the path. One of your officers
should look for it when they have a chance."

Gambrelli continued to walk through the cottage, occasionally sitting in a chair or leaning against
a doorway. Several times he wandered in and out of

the building. The police officer took up his original position at the kitchen table, leaving the silent inspector to wander around in circles alone.

In the bedroom for the fourth or fifth time, Gambrelli examined the photographs displayed in plain, wooden frames on top of the dresser. One was of Prosecutor Bertrand standing next to the cottage holding a bottle of wine, the sea visible in the distance. The next was of Bertrand and a young woman Gambrelli assumed to be Annette Cuomo, standing on a narrow footbridge. The woman had a beauty beyond that of simple youth. He felt an unmistakable air of sensuality exuding from her, even in this snapshot. Bertrand, his arm wrapped about her waist, looked as if he had not a care in the world. Behind them was a cathedral spire. Gambrelli studied the structure for a moment before he recognized it as the east tower of Sacred Heart on the canal bank near the University District.

A third photograph was not in a frame, but lay flat on the dresser. It was of a woman younger than Annette, but identical in her features and her beauty. The young woman was sitting cross-legged on a plaid blanket next to a wicker basket. She was dappled in light and shade from a large tree not visible in the picture.

Gambrelli placed this third photograph in his coat pocket. He believed it was of the younger sister, Lisa, who sooner or later would have to be interrogated.

*   *   *

Gambrelli stopped at a tobacconist on his way to Annette Cuomo's shop and bought two packs of cigarettes. Then he walked another block to where the officer assigned to guard the art shop was awaiting his arrival.

Thoughtfully, as though contemplating a purchase, Gambrelli moved about the shop. He first inspected the items for sale and the paintings on the walls, noting that the majority of them were signed by Major Ormond's witness, Joseph Krantz.

In the rear storage room, Gambrelli removed two ledgers from a desk drawer and carefully examined them. He replaced the ledgers and took a handful of letters from the top drawer of the desk. All the letters were addressed in the same hand and bore a return address of *L.C. number 27, Leopold Street*.

Gambrelli called to the officer who was still standing at the entrance to the shop. "Call your headquarters and have Joseph Krantz brought here to me."

While he waited, Gambrelli read the letters. They were all from the victim's sister, Lisa Cuomo. None of them contained anything of consequence. When he finished, he placed them in the desk drawer as he had found them. Then he took a souvenir ashtray from a shelf in the sales room and carried it into the back room.

As he lit a cigarette, a policeman arrived with Krantz in tow. Gambrelli indicated a chair near the desk where the officer deposited the witness.

"Would you like me to stay?" The officer asked.

Gambrelli assessed Krantz who was leaning forward with his head bowed.

"No, I think we will be fine."

"The Major said when you are done with him he is free to go...unless you think otherwise."

Once the officer was gone Gambrelli sat behind the desk and waited until Krantz looked at him.

"Were you Annette Cuomo's lover?"

"No. I told the police—"

"I know what you told the police. Now I want you to tell me. She was a beautiful woman, the type I am sure is rare on the island. You are her age. Both of you are interested in the arts. I should think it a natural combination." Gambrelli offered a cigarette.

"One could only hope." Krantz took the cigarette, struck a match, and wiped his brow. "But she was already in love with Bertrand."

"Do you know him?"

"I was introduced to him once, a few months ago...but no I did not really know him. Other than things Annette may have said. She talked of him often. She loved him, of that I can be most certain."

"Did that anger you, a young, desirable woman rejecting you for a much older man—a married man—who only occasionally visited, leaving you to provide companionship for her in his absence?"

"That's not it at all. We were friends. She wanted to introduce me to her sister, Lisa."

"And did she?"

"No. Lisa was to move to the island a few months ago, but for one reason or another, it never happened."

"How often did you see Annette?"

"Almost every day. I'd often come in to see how the sale of my work was going and to drop off new paintings or note cards she ordered. Most afternoons, I'd bring her mail from the post office."

"How often did she receive mail from her sister?" Gambrelli put out his cigarette and pulled the letters from the desk.

"Once a week. I brought her one yesterday, just before she locked up and went home."

"Did she take the letter with her when she left?"

"No, she read it and put in the top desk drawer with the others."

"Think, Joseph. Are you sure?" Gambrelli examined the envelopes. None of them had been postmarked in the last week; the most recent one had been mailed from the City two weeks earlier.

"I'm sure. Annette was sitting at the desk when I gave her the letter. She opened the envelope, took out the letter, and read it while I sat exactly where I am now." Krantz put out his cigarette. "And there was a key. In the letter, there was a key from her sister."

"What did she do with the key?"

"She put it on her key chain with the key to the shop and the new one for her house."

"And she took the keys with her?" Gambrelli placed the letters in the desk drawer.

"Yes. How else could she have locked the shop door, or opened the door to her cottage?"

"You saw her do that?"

"Yes." Krantz appeared to be growing tired of answering seemingly silly questions. "I saw her lock the shop, and I walked her home where I saw her unlock her door."

"Look around the shop. Is everything in its normal order? Is this the way things looked yesterday at closing time?"

Krantz moved around the storage room, and then walked out to the front of the shop before returning to Gambrelli. "The shop looks the same, but the boxes along the back wall were not open as they are now, and they were all against the wall, not pushed out in the middle of the floor. And the cabinet doors were closed yesterday," he said, waving his hand at a row of wooden storage lockers along the wall opposite the desk.

Gambrelli called to the officer on duty and obtained his statement. No police search of the premises had been conducted.

"Well someone apparently tossed things about looking for something. Make a note of that, Officer, and advise Major Ormond...By the way...when you first arrived here was the front door locked?"

"No, it was closed but not locked."

Gambrelli stepped around the desk and placed a thick arm across Krantz's narrow shoulders.

"Come with me, Joseph. Let us have a drink and talk some more."

Gambrelli filled Krantz's glass and placed the wine bottle on the table. The café was cool, and what few customers there were paid little attention to the chain-smoking witness and investigator scribbling in his notebook.

"So ..." Gambrelli put down his pen. "Last week, when she returned from the City, Annette was full of plans to expand her shop and turn it into a real art gallery. Yet three days ago, Sunday, she told you she was leaving the island. And just yesterday, she said she was going to tell Bertrand she never wanted to see him again."

Krantz nodded.

"And it was Sunday that she had the brass bolt installed on her cottage door?"

"Yes, Chief Inspector. If you doubt it, you can check with the locksmith, Walter Maurel. His shop is just down the street." Krantz took a sip of wine and lit another cigarette. "It was Sunday afternoon. I saw Maurel's bicycle leaning against Annette's house as I was passing along Beach Road. When I got to the house, he was just finishing up. She paid him, we drank a glass of wine, and he left. It was then that Annette told me she planned to leave the island."

"Did she ever explain why the sudden change in plans?"

"No...I asked, but..."

"And the new lock? Did she say why she needed to have it installed with such immediacy?"

"No...but I had suggested it to her several times."

"I have examined the account books. The shop was losing money. How could she have had the resources to expand the shop?"

"She had cash. She showed me last Wednesday, the day she came back from the City. I don't know how much she had, but it was at least several thousand francs.

"Did she say where it came from?"

"She said she had collected her back pay from a former employer. I suspected she had gotten it from Bertrand, but I didn't say so."

"Other than Bertrand, did you ever see Annette in the company of another man?"

"Customers in the gallery, other shop owners along the street...but if you mean socially, having dinner or drinks with a man, Bertrand was the only one who I know of."

"Do you think she would have told you if there was another man in her life?"

"I'm certain of it."

"Her key chain, what did it look like?"

"A brass ring with three keys, one for the shop, and one for the new lock on her cottage door, and the key from her sister that came yesterday in the letter. And there was a chain attached to the ring ... with a small, brass seahorse on the end."

"Did Annette make a habit of leaving the island, maybe to return to the City or somewhere else?"

"No. Since the day she opened the shop, she'd never left, except for last Tuesday."

"Are you certain?" Gambrelli asked.

"I am positive, Chief Inspector." Krantz reached for the wine.

"But you said you saw her 'almost every day'. That would mean there were days when you did not see her."

"I'd meant I visited her almost every day. On the days when I did not stop in, I would wave to her through the shop window."

"Every day?"

"It's possible there may have been a day... Maybe a few when I did not see her ..."

Gambrelli closed his notebook and left Krantz to finish the bottle.

. . .

He walked along the street until he came to the locksmith's. Inside the shop, a customer was waiting for an elderly man wearing a blue smock to file the edges of a newly cut key. When the customer departed, Gambrelli stepped to the counter.

"Monsieur Maurel, I'd like to ask you about a brass bolt you installed on Annette Cuomo's cottage door on Sunday."

The locksmith took a pair of wire-rimmed spectacles from his workbench and pushed them onto the bridge of his nose.

"Are you with the police? I don't recognize you."

Gambrelli took his identity card from his jacket and handed it to the locksmith, who read the card aloud.

"Gambrelli, Chief Inspector, Metropolitan Police." He handed the card back. "They got a lot of you Italians in the Metropolitan Police?"

"We have a lot of everybody in the department. Did you install a brass bolt on Cuomo's door?"

"Chief Inspector. That's a pretty high position. Your parents both Italian?"

"They were French."

"Gambrelli…That's not a French name, it's Italian."

He suppressed the urge to reach across the counter and grab the locksmith by the ear. When the urge passed he smiled. "My father's family moved to France over a hundred years ago."

"And your mother?"

"My mother was English."

The locksmith grunted and removed his glasses. Gambrelli assumed the grunt was a display of satisfaction that English blood explained his position.

"You're old enough to have been in the War."

"I served for a while," Gambrelli said.

"It took my son. Left my wife and me to care for his widow and boy." The locksmith placed his glasses back on the workbench. "Now the boy is a man and the Hun is on the move again. How much longer do you think it will be?"

"Before what?"

"Before the German makes his move." The locksmith laid his hands on the counter. "Some say the German people will not go again against the world. What do you say?"

"I hope it will never happen again."

"But you fear it will. I can see it in your eyes, and hear it in your voice."

Gambrelli made no attempt to respond.

"My wife is German," the locksmith said. He took his glasses from the bench and tapped them against the counter. "She says it is going to happen soon." He slid the glasses into a shirt pocket. "Is your wife Italian?"

"No, Austrian." Gambrelli, who never wore a wedding ring, wondered how the old man guessed he was married.

"Then she knows. If she's an Austrian, it's in her blood, she can sense it. What does she say?"

"I've never discussed it with her."

The locksmith's clouded grey eyes blinked at Gambrelli in disbelief. "The Hun would be the perfect citizen in a perfect world. He trusts his government. It is impossible for him to think his leaders would lie and deceive." The locksmith pushed some tools to the corner of the workbench apparently unable to refrain from constantly moving something about. "They're not like us, my friend. We trust no one… politicians and generals least of all. The world is not perfect; it is chaos, deceit, lies, and illusion." He grabbed Gambrelli's wrist. "We are the perfect citizens for this world."

Gambrelli pulled his wrist free with a gentle twist. "My friend, I hear what you are saying. Now did you install a brass bolt on the door of Annette Cuomo's cottage?"

"I installed the bolt. Best quality available," the locksmith said softly, with no indication he had been oozing white froth from the corners of his mouth just moments before. "And I did it at a fair price considering it was Sunday. She came to my home, said it had to be done right away, couldn't wait until Monday. She paid me in full. Nice girl. Even threw in extra, since it was the Sabbath."

"Did she say why she needed it to be done right away?"

"She said Sunday was her only day off."

"Were you replacing an old lock?"

"No, the door never had one. And the wood was as hard as iron. I worked up quite a sweat getting the holes drilled."

"How many keys did you make for the lock?"

"Two...but she wanted three...I left her with one and brought the other back here to cut a duplicate." He turned to search the work bench. "I've got it here...I was going to make the copy and drop it at her shop today."

"Where's the post office?"

"Around the corner ... in the back of the pharmacy."

"Your friend Krantz is at the café down the street, sitting alone with more than a half bottle of good wine, already paid for, and what's left of a pack of my cigarettes."

Thirty paces down the street, Gambrelli looked over his shoulder in time to see the locksmith leaving his shop and heading toward the café.

*   *   *

At the rear of the pharmacy was a small alcove, hardly more than a closet. Behind the counter, a tall, thin man in a white medical coat was shuffling letters into pigeonholes along the wall. The man was close to eighty, and his gnarled fingers had some difficulty in separating the envelopes.

Gambrelli leaned on the counter without speaking. The man ignored him, even though his presence was apparent. Finally, Gambrelli cleared his throat. "How long does it take for a letter posted in the City to reach the island?" Gambrelli asked.

The man in the white coat did not turn from his task. "Just a minute, I'm busy."

Gambrelli lit a cigarette and blew the smoke at the back of the white coat.

After the last letter was tucked into its proper place the elderly man turned his attention to the stranger who was filling his tiny space with yellow clouds of smoke.

"Now what is it that you need, young man?"

"How long does—"

"Yes, I heard you the first time. Two days, maybe three at the most."

"What time of day does the mail arrive?"

"It comes in on the noon ferry. I get it on my way back from lunch and have it sorted and ready for pick up by two."

"So a letter that arrived from the City yesterday, Tuesday, would have been posted ...?"

"Three days at the most." The twisted fingers reached for another stack of letters.

"Where is the hospital?" Gambrelli asked.

"At the end of South Street." The pharmacist shuffled the envelopes without looking at Gambrelli. "Do you need any stamps?"

*　*　*

The coroner was unavailable, so his assistant pulled the sheet back for Gambrelli's inspection of Annette Cuomo's body. After two minutes, Gambrelli began to make notes in his book.

"These bruises on either clavicle ..." Gambrelli pointed with his pen. "What did the coroner make of them?"

"Let me see." The assistant leafed through the coroner's report. "It says they were probably made by the murderer pulling the victim down from behind and holding her on the bed."

"And how does a man hold a woman down by both of her shoulders while he is stabbing her?" Gambrelli lit a cigarette.

"I don't know—"

"I wasn't talking to you. How long have you worked for the coroner?"

"Are you talking to me now?"

"I'm certainly not talking to her." Gambrelli pulled the sheet further back exposing the corpse in full.

"Three years."

"And in that time, how many deaths by stabbing have you seen?"

"Two. Both were victims of drunken brawls between fishermen."

"And these small wounds on her chest and stomach, what did your boss make of them?"

"Hesitation marks," the assistant read. "The killer had to work himself up to the point where he could deliver the killing strike."

"And where did the coroner get the expertise to come up with that idea?"

"From a conference he attended last fall, a national conference in Paris," the assistant said. "He showed me his notes from a lecture where the issue had been presented."

"Did his notes also reflect that hesitation marks gradually get deeper as the pattern progresses?"

He took the report from the assistant then pointed with his cigarette toward Cuomo's body. "It is written here that all of the smaller wounds are of approximately the same depth."

Gambrelli flicked ashes on the floor while the assistant read the report and examined the wounds with the intensity of a good student. When the assistant's inspection was complete, he looked up at Gambrelli. "If not hesitation marks, then what are they?" the assistant asked.

"Have the coroner check his notes again." Gambrelli headed for the door. "If there is no mention of wounds inflicted during interrogation by torture, then he missed the second part of my lecture."

NINE

Major Ormond placed his hands on top of the investigative file. His fingers tapped nervously on the document folder as he waited for Gambrelli to finish speaking.

"Now Major, I have told you everything that I have seen, and all that I have heard."

"Nothing you have said proves Bertrand is innocent. We have all we need to charge him with the murder."

"It's what you don't have that is of concern to me." Gambrelli paced in front of the major's desk.

"What don't we have? Some keys, a letter, a bottle of champagne, possibly some missing money? These are of little consequence compared to the evidence against Bertrand."

"They are things we cannot explain; therefore, they are of great consequence, Major." Gambrelli stopped his pacing. "Why would Bertrand take the keys? He has his own, a duplicate for the shop."

"Precisely. He may have taken them to make us look for someone else."

"But an extra set of keys were not recovered from his person, or in the search of his hotel room."

"He could have thrown them away, along with the bottle of champagne and the letter." Major Ormond was firm, looking satisfied with his response.

"Then why not throw away the bloody shirt?"

"Perhaps he intended to dispose of it later, never anticipating that the body would be discovered so soon. My men were on him in a flash."

"Why leave his tie, still binding the victim's wrists? Bertrand has prosecuted a hundred murderers. He is no stranger to evidence and the trail a murderer leaves behind." Gambrelli paced back and forth again, a caged bear unaccustomed to subjugation.

"Precisely."

Gambrelli glared at the repetition of the word. Nothing was precise.

"Knowing we would think him above such a foolish oversight, he may have intentionally left the clue," Ormond said.

"Do you hear yourself, Major? 'May have,' 'could have,' 'perhaps' … those are not the words upon which a man can be asked to surrender his life."

"And for the lack of explanation as to the whereabouts of a few trivial items are we to allow a murder suspect to walk away from justice?"

Gambrelli did not answer. He lit a cigarette and leaned against the wall, wiping sweat from his brow with the back of his hand.

"In the face of the evidence, do you deny it is possible that Prosecutor Bertrand killed the Cuomo woman?" Ormond asked.

"Anything is possible. I just find it unlikely."

"The mayor and the deputy prosecutor want Bertrand charged immediately," Ormond said in a quiet tone.

"What's the rush?"

"This is not the City, Chief Inspector. We are not accustomed to having murderers running about. This island survives on tourist dollars. How long will it be before every newspaper in the country cries out that there is a maniac loose on the Island of Q, slashing women in the night? The business community is demanding the mayor resolve this immediately."

"We are not politicians or shopkeepers, Major. We are policemen. It will serve you well to remember that." Gambrelli picked up his coat.

"Twenty-four hours, Gambrelli; that is all I can delay. Then I will bring the evidence against Bertrand to the Examining Magistrate."

"I am leaving on the first ferry in the morning. I should be back in the city by ten. Give me some time to sort things out."

TEN

The proprietor of the Island Tavern hovered over Gambrelli's table, pouring a second glass of white wine from a sweating ceramic pitcher.

"How is the investigation going, Chief Inspector?"

Gambrelli ignored the question and took a long drink of the cold wine. He was in a foul mood. He did not like being placed on a timetable, even if it was Major Ormond's problem. *Let him charge Bertrand*, he thought. Ormond's the one who will have to explain later that he arrested the wrong man. Or, maybe Bertrand did kill the woman and Ormond was right. It was too soon to know.

"Is the grilled swordfish to your liking? The olive oil and capers are from Spain. They add something special, don't you think?"

"What is the celebration over there?" Gambrelli poked his chin in the direction of a group of fishermen gathered at the end of the bar.

"Oh, Claude Beluse, the small, dark one in the blue shirt, is buying a few rounds for the men." The proprietor sat at an empty table to Gambrelli's left.

"What's the occasion?" Gambrelli tried to hide his irritation at having an uninvited guest at his elbow. "Successful fishing trip?"

"Claude can't fish for the love of Judas. He just collected on an old gambling debt. He came in an hour ago and paid off his tab. Two months of wine and meals. I was just about to cut him off for good when he showed up and laid cash on the bar."

"It must be hard to spend your life on the sea if you can't catch fish." Gambrelli took another bite of swordfish. "The oil and capers are excellent."

"Claude has only fished for a few years. Before that, he was a maintenance man for hotels in the center of town. I think he still works for a few of them on occasion."

Gambrelli slowly sipped the wine as the vaguest thread of a thought attached itself to the edges of his mind.

"Was he ever employed at the Parc Hotel?"

"Yes, that is where he worked before buying his fishing boat."

He took a hard look at Claude Beluse. The small man in the blue shirt did not have the manner of his companions. His skin was tan but not weathered like the rest of them.

The chief inspector returned to his meal. Occasionally he sensed that Beluse was looking at him, but every time he turned in the direction of the bois-terous party, Beluse quickly looked away.

"They know who you are," the proprietor said.

"Is that because you told them?" Gambrelli took another mouthful of the grilled fish.

"I may have mentioned that you are a friend, likely to stop by for dinner."

"Do you have a phone I could use, maybe in the back room, away from the crowd?"

"Certainly, Chief Inspector." The proprietor puffed up with importance, obviously proud to as-sist in the investigation. "I will lead the way. It's through the kitchen, in my office."

"I'll find my own way. Watch my plate." Gam-brelli stood and pulled himself to his full height. He deliberately lumbered in the direction of Claude Beluse, walking directly toward the center of the man's chest.

Beluse struggled to maintain his ground, but at the last moment, he stepped aside, not lifting his eyes to meet the chief inspector's accusatory stare. Gambrelli stopped in front of him and placed a strong grip on Beluse's shoulder. The man squirmed, but Gambrelli held fast. Finally, Beluse looked up to meet the policeman's ice-blue stare.

"Where is the men's room?" Gambrelli asked without a hint of humanity.

Beluse pointed to the rear of the tavern, and Gambrelli released his grip and walked away.

In the tiny office, Gambrelli wiped the greasy phone receiver against his coat. He directed the operator to connect him to Metropolitan Police Headquarters in the City, where Detective Sergeant Christian Andres carefully wrote down Gambrelli's instructions.

"Put whoever is available on this. I want as many answers as possible waiting for me. Clear your schedule, you will accompany me for the interviews. Pick me up at Central Station. I will be on the first train from the coast."

Gambrelli spoke to the operator again.

"Connect me to the Provincial Police."

"Is there a problem at the Island Tavern?" the operator asked.

"Connect the damn call, and don't linger on the line this time, Madame, or I will have you arrested for interfering with police matters."

The major was not in. Gambrelli left the name Claude Beluse for the major to check on in the morning.

Gambrelli finished his meal and another glass of wine. The proprietor busied himself with the other customers, but made a special effort to bid the chief inspector a good night.

As Gambrelli stepped onto the tavern's veranda, he caught a glimpse of the little one-clawed crab chasing a larger cousin. The larger crab, despite having the advantage of two claws, was in full retreat, backing along the edge of the wooden deck. The challenger fell, or might have been pushed, off the edge. In victory, the little crab slowly returned to his position under the café table.

"You're the only one I will miss when I'm gone," Gambrelli said.

The invalid crab advanced toward Gambrelli's shoe, and he gave the one-armed warrior a gentle nudge goodbye.

THE TIMES

Milan, September 6

Warning from Il Duce:
NO WEAK STOMACHS

...there cannot be weak stomachs within the ranks of the Fascist Party. "We say, we repeat, we cry out, that Fascist Italy must be militarist. Militarist is the nation that subordinates to the military necessities everything else of the material and moral life of the individual as well as of the community."

6 SEPTEMBER

The City

ELEVEN

Detective Sergeant Andres handed Gambrelli the appointment book from Prosecutor Bertrand's office. As he flipped through the pages, Andres pulled the unmarked police car into the heavy city traffic. A cold rain pelted the windshield.

"Where to first, Chief?" Andres asked.

Gambrelli checked his notebook. On the train from the coast, he had read over his interview of Prosecutor Bertrand and made a list of people and places that would guide the initial inquiry. "The Savage Gallery."

Gambrelli lit a cigarette and rolled the window down. He welcomed the cool air and smell of the rain.

"Any luck finding the sister, Lisa Cuomo?"

"Gavros is on it. I told him once he finds her to call the bureau and stay with her until we arrive."

Gambrelli watched the city roll by. Gavros was a good choice. At twenty-five, he was the youngest of Gambrelli's detectives, olive skinned, handsome, and single; he would have no trouble keeping Lisa Cuomo entertained and happily waiting. That is, of course, if Gavros found her.

For a moment, Gambrelli considered assigning another detective to assist in the search for the girl. If he was right and Annette Cuomo's murderer was searching for something he did not find on the Island of Q, then Lisa may also be in grave danger.

"Is something wrong Chief?" Andres asked.

"No, just thinking it might be better to assign additional men to search for Lisa Cuomo." Gambrelli blew smoke toward the window.

"Lanier and Bruno are still at the office. I could send one of them."

"Yes, maybe later. Let's wait and see how Gavros does."

 .   .   .

There were no customers in the Savage Gallery when Gambrelli arrived. He shook the rain from his coat as he was greeted by the smiling manager, a thin, pale woman in her mid-forties. The manager's pleasant manner did not dissipate when he presented his identification and introduced Sergeant Andres.

"Ah, Annette. You have no idea how many times I have wished she was still working here," the manager said. "She is all right, isn't she?"

"When was the last time you saw her?" Gambrelli asked.

"It was Wednesday, last week. She was waiting outside for me to open the gallery. I know it
was a Wednesday, because that's the day we get our
frames delivered."

"What did she want? Why was she here?"

"She said she had some packages to wrap and
wanted to borrow some of our materials in the
packing room. I said of course she could and left
her to her business."

"What was she packaging?"

"I have no idea. I did not ask." The manager
led Gambrelli to the back room, leaving Andres behind. "She left with several small bundles sticking
out from a black canvas bag she put in her leather
shoulder bag..." The manager hesitated as if something she had not intended to say had almost slipped
out.

"What is it?" Gambrelli asked.

"Nothing...well something odd..."

"Go on."

"She made me promise not to tell anyone she
had been here."

"Did she say who might inquire?"

"No, and I was so surprised by her request that
I didn't ask."

"When did she leave?"

"Well, I opened at nine, so I guess about nine
thirty."

"Did anyone come in looking for her?" Gambrelli made some notes.

"Yes. How did you guess?" The manager pulled gently on a gold chain that framed the neckline of her black dress. "A terrible man, a former employer of Annette's, came in looking for her at about ten. I was so glad she was already gone. When he arrived I realized why she had wanted her visit to remain a secret."

"Do you know his name?"

"Philippe. Annette rarely talked of him, but each time she did, she would tremble. I saw him accost her once on the street after we closed the gallery. I was headed the other way but turned in time to see him push her against the building near the corner. I started to go to her aid, but they walked off. I mentioned it to Annette the next day. She said he had a bad temper but meant nothing by it, so I let it drop."

"Philippe, who? Do you know his last name?"

"No, she never told me."

"Where was it that she worked for him?"

"Somewhere near the harbor, a warehouse of some sort. She was a bookkeeper...."

"What did this Philippe say last Wednesday?"

"He came in, walked right up to the counter, and said, 'Where is Annette? Has that bitch been here?' I'm sorry, Chief Inspector, but those were his exact words. I told him I had not seen her in months, but he walked though the back rooms looking for her, shouting her name. Then he took a one-hundred-franc note from his pocket, wrote a phone number on it, and told me to call him 'if that thieving whore shows her face.' His words, not mine."

"Was anyone else present when he came in?"

"Yes, Madame Bertrand was here in the gallery. She had come in a few minutes earlier. I had been tempted to tell her I had just seen Annette, since the Bertrands were such good customers and bought exclusively from Annette. Thank God I hadn't said anything. I can't imagine dragging the Bertrands into anything to do with that beast Philippe."

"Did Madame Bertrand speak to you after Philippe left?"

"No, she hurried out of the gallery as soon as he was gone. She must have been appalled by the scene."

"I will need the phone number from the hundred-franc note," Gambrelli said. "In fact I will need the note itself." He reached into his wallet and counted out one hundred francs in smaller denomination notes, exchanging them for the single note supplied by Philippe.

Sergeant Andres waited in the car. Gambrelli crossed the street to the booksellers shop. Once inside he confirmed that Bertrand could have easily observed the comings and goings from the Gallery and by leaning against the shelves on the wall furthest from the shop entrance he would have been able to watch his wife and the belligerent Philippe enter the taxi at the end of the block and drive off.

On the first try the passenger door bounced off Gambrelli shoulder. He slid toward the sergeant and pulled the door again. It shut securely.

"What was that about?"

"The door...it wouldn't close."

"I mean running across the street to the book shop."

"Nothing...curiosity...nothing."

Sergeant Andres shifted the car into gear and shrugged. Another oddity left unexplained. Over the years he had become accustomed to the chief inspector's insensitivity to the desire of others to understand what was happening around them.

TWELVE

The polished parquet floors of the University Club were partially protected by precisely placed Oriental carpets. Gambrelli's eyes followed the flow of mahogany pillars and archways that carved their way along the corridors leading to the various sitting areas and dining rooms. The heavy smell of roasting lamb and duck floated from the unseen kitchens, overpowering the scent of cigar smoke and brandy coming from the massive library to his left. The Island Tavern's swordfish, swimming in Spanish olive oil and capers, was a distant memory as Gambrelli's stomach began to growl.

The logs in the entry hall fireplace crackled and hissed. Before breakfast, Gambrelli escaped the sweltering heat of the island. Now, just before noon, he was tempted to move closer to the flames to take the chill of the city's dampness from his bones.

He leaned on the corner of the mahogany reception desk and waited patiently as the maître d' referred to a leather-bound reservation book. Each turning of the vellum pages reinforced his unspoken attitude that the police were interrupting him with concerns far less important that his own. Gambrelli was sure that had an officer of lower rank presented himself at lunchtime, he would have been told to return later in the afternoon for the required information.

Gambrelli was glad he had left Andres to wait in the car. The sergeant's patience would have evaporated about the time the man turned his nose up at the sight of the police identification card. Gambrelli was certain that, by now, Andres would have had the head of the maître d' securely wedged between the sergeant's heavy fist and the top of the mahogany reception desk.

"Here it is," the maître d' said. "I told you I was sure the Bertrands had been here last month, on Saturday the 25th. It was the night of the charity banquet to benefit the new wing of the Hôtel Dieu."

Gambrelli turned the book and read the entries. "There are no names listed for the banquet."

"Certainly not. Only the event is listed. The guest list is attached to the seating chart in my office. I can get it if you'd like, but I distinctly remember Madame Bertrand standing behind this desk reviewing the list and chart with me. She was on the fund-raising committee and was attending to several of the final details that evening."

"And would this book have been on the desk at that time?"

"The reservation book is always on this desk."

"And on that Saturday, it would have been opened just as you have it now?"

"Yes."

"So it would have been easy for Madame Bertrand to have seen that her husband had lunch here on Friday, the 24th, with Monsieur Goddard, the divorce attorney?"

"If she had been inclined to read the reservation book, yes, I suppose."

"Keep track of the book and the banquet paperwork. I may need to have one of my men take them into evidence."

Gambrelli inhaled a last breath of roasted lamb before stepping out into the rain just as Sergeant Andres was walking back to the car from the police call box on the corner.

"Inspector Renard ran the information we have on Philippe past his old partners in the Narcotics Bureau. They are looking for a photo of a guy they think fits the bill. It will be an old photo, from an old arrest, but it should do."

"Have Renard take the photo—"

"As soon as he gets it he'll be on his way to the gallery to talk to the manager. He called her, and she agreed to wait for his arrival."

"You have the address for Madame Julienne Vercel?" Gambrelli said, reading from the list in his notebook.

Andres nodded and pulled a slip of paper from the pocket of his wet coat.

As the police car pulled from the curb, Gambrelli cast a glance at the steaming windows of the University Club, wondering if it was the scent of lamb or duck pressing against the panes trying to escape.

THIRTEEN

The Vercel estate occupied six hectares of the lush North Gate District at the edge of the City. The canopy of elm trees that sheltered the road from the pelting rain gave way to an open expanse of lawn and manicured gardens. Gambrelli flicked a cigarette butt out the window as Sergeant Andres swung the car onto the crushed limestone drive leading to the main house.

Small puddles of rainwater formed at their feet as droplets fell from their coats onto the marble floor of the entryway. Gambrelli felt uncharacteristically ill at ease, shifting his weight from one foot to the other as they waited for the butler to announce their arrival. Before Andres could inquire if something was wrong, Julienne Vercel appeared in the archway of the sitting room, her light brown hair pulled back in a bun, her trim figure accentuated by a dark green dress of mandarin design.

For a moment she hesitated. "My God, Arthur, is it you?" Then she rushed toward Gambrelli, throwing her arms about his neck and fairly leaping into his arms. "I can't believe it."

The chief inspector looked past her cheek at Andres, feeling the flush of blood rising to color his face. Julienne Vercel released her arms and landed squarely in front of the flustered chief inspector. She took both his hands in hers, and for a moment, Gambrelli thought she was going to kiss his fingers.

"My hero." She pulled his hands to her chest then looked at Andres. "He saved my life, you know."

"Julienne, this is Detective Sergeant Andres." Gambrelli pulled his hands free and attempted to regain his composure.

Andres extended his hand, only to find himself being pulled by the arm into the sitting room along with Gambrelli, Julienne swaying between them.

"What has it been, Arthur, twenty years?"

She placed Andres into a high-back, leather chair before pushing Gambrelli onto a couch near the fire and, still holding his hand, dropped next to him leaving not the slightest space between them.

"Oh, my God, I can't believe you're here. Wait 'til I tell the other girls. They will just die of jealousy. We follow all your exploits in the newspaper. My God, you are quite the celebrity. All those horrible murders, all these years; I don't know how you cope. And you must do something about the photographs they print of you. They're so unflattering." Turning to Andres while leaning on Gambrelli's left shoulder, she asked, "Has he ever told you of the night he saved six girls from certain death?"

"Really, Julienne," Gambrelli interrupted. "The detective sergeant and I have—"

"Don't be impatient, Arthur. You want to hear the story, don't you, Detective Sergeant?"

"Yes, I most certainly do." Andres smiled at Gambrelli.

"There, see Arthur? Now just relax. Let me take your coat." She pulled at his lapel.

"That won't be necessary." Gambrelli pulled back.

"You haven't changed. All business." She theatrically kissed his cheek before he could pull away. "Grumpy." She pushed against his shoulder. "Sergeant, please remove that wet coat."

Julienne took a cigarette from a black lacquered box on the table then inserted it into an ivory holder. Gambrelli pulled a lighter from his pocket and lit her cigarette, and then lit one of his own.

Julienne crossed her legs and with a wave of her cigarette turned her captivating smile toward Sergeant Andres. "There were six of us girls, all actresses and dancers. I was the youngest, barely seventeen, living in a rooming house on St. Germaine. The place was rundown at the corners to say the least, but the rent was cheap and we had no money. The landlord was a vile man, always creeping about and pressing his watery eye to the keyhole. But we got used to it and considered it fair exchange for the reduced rent.

"It was about this time of year; the weather had turned cold, the rain pounding, the windows leaking. The War had begun, but its horror had not yet reached us. We were huddled, two to a bed, under thin blankets. I awoke in the middle of the night to Arthur's thunderous voice saying, 'Police. There is a fire,'" she said in a grave baritone, imitating the chief inspector. "It was quite alarming. 'Get up!' he'd said, as he scooped me into his arms and threw me over his shoulder." She pulled Gambrelli's arm tight against her side.

The gaunt figure of the butler, who had greeted the detectives at the front door, appeared in the archway of the sitting room.

"Monsieur Garnier, please tell Doreen we will have tea ... and some small cakes for our guests," Julienne said softly. "So there we were, shivering in the cold rain, crying, wrapped in blankets. Firemen were rushing about, the rooming house ablaze against the dark of night. Then the police loaded us into a milk wagon and took us to an inn on the north end of the *presqu'ile*. Remember that night?" She looked at Gambrelli, who was reclining, abdicating all control of the situation to her enthusiasm.

He smiled and nodded.

"It was quite a sight, Sergeant," she continued. "The innkeeper, a wonderful old man...he looked like Père Noël. Didn't he?" She looked to Gambrelli who responded with a shrug. "Well he did to me." Turning back to Andres she continued determined not to lose the mood. "Ignore him. So the innkeeper stoked the fireplace, and we sat along a huge wooden table, all of us drenched within an inch of our lives. Arthur came down the stairs; his arms piled high with dry blankets, and a good thing because we were in our nightgowns, which were at best a bit skimpy."

She smiled at Gambrelli, who immediately averted his eyes as tea and cakes were set on the low table before them.

"And then David came from the back room with a basket full of bottles. My God, I've never drunk so much wine. After a few bottles, some of the firemen arrived, their faces charred black, smelling of smoke. I'll tell you, Sergeant, you may think I'm mad, but it was so much fun. To this day, I don't think I've ever laughed and cried so much."

She laid a hand on Gambrelli's leg as she continued looking at Andres, whose face betrayed his fascination with this glimpse of history.

"It was David who started dancing, wasn't it?" she asked Gambrelli who, determined not to encourage her, did not respond. "Anyway, soon the blankets were off and we were dancing. I kept glancing across the room at Arthur, who refused to participate in the festivities, much in the way he is acting now."

She squeezed his thigh, and he jerked it away, shooting her a disapproving glance, which she met with a smile.

"There he was, standing at the bar all by himself, sipping a glass of calvados, his big arms folded across his chest. He looked so magnificent in his dark blue uniform, those gold and red sergeant's stripes stretched across his biceps. All the girls fell for him."

Sergeant Andres looked at Gambrelli as if seeing him for the first time, the question on his lips muted by Gambrelli's glare, a stern warning to keep silent. But after a bite of cake, the sergeant asked, "Who is David?"

"Your police commissioner, David DeMartell," she answered, then turned to Gambrelli. "I saw David last month at the Pearson wedding. He must have told you."

"He mentioned it," Gambrelli said.

"He still loves to dance. And after all these years, he still has that mischievous twinkle in his eye." She smiled and sipped her tea. "It's hard to believe you two ruffians have risen through the ranks. Why, I remember the time—"

"Julienne," Gambrelli interrupted, "we are here to ask you about last Tuesday night. You were at the Rinaldi Theatre with Adele Bertrand."

"And several others. We always—"

"Yes, we know. When you left the theatre, where did you go to dinner?"

"To the Café des Artistes. We took a taxi, although we could have walked; it was late, and as you know, the streets at that time of night are not the safest. No offense to the police."

"The café is to the west of the theatre." Gambrelli took his notebook from his inside pocket. "Are you sure you did not travel east?"

"I don't remember." She set her cup on the low table in front of her. "We drove around for a little while. We were giving a ride to Jean Louis Tremont... the actor... I'm sure you must know him. After the performance, we went backstage. Jean Louis is an old friend of mine, and Adele wanted to ask him if he would do a reading for one of her charity luncheons. He was most gracious."

"Where did you take him?"

"To some restaurant; he was meeting someone. I really don't remember, I was so busy chatting."

"Yes, hard to believe." Gambrelli jotted a note. "Did you notice any change in Adele Bertrand's disposition during the evening, possibly after the taxi ride?"

"Odd you should say that. Yes, I did notice when we arrived at the café, she was in quite a down mood. I even called her the next day to see if she was ill. She said she was fine ... then hurried me off the phone. Quite unlike her, I would say."

"And the night before last, Tuesday night, was Adele Bertrand with you as usual?"

"No, she was under the weather and begged off."

"Well, Julienne, we must be going." Gambrelli stood abruptly and motioned to Andres before their hostess could raise an objection. The trio made their way to the door.

"Please do not discuss our visit with anyone, especially Adele Bertrand," Gambrelli said as he swung open the heavy front door.

"Why, Arthur, I assure you, I have no idea what you are investigating, nor do I want to know. I will be the soul of discretion."

"I'm sure," he said.

"Detective Sergeant, are you married?" she asked.

"Yes, I am."

"Well then, you and your wife are invited to my Christmas party this year. I will send an invitation to Police Headquarters for you." She looked at Gambrelli. "And one for you and your wife too. All the girls will be here, and I'm sure they will be dying to meet Madame Gambrelli, the woman we have all been jealous of these past decades." She gave him a kiss on each cheek. "David and his wonderful wife will be here, so please, Arthur, don't be your recalcitrant self and refuse to come. Besides, my husband would love to meet the man who saved my life." She winked at Gambrelli and closed the door.

"The Rinaldi Theatre," Gambrelli said as they drove onto the main road.

"My wife will be excited to attend the Vercel's Christmas party," Andres said as he turned on the windshield wipers.

Gambrelli did not comment.

"You will be going, won't you, Chief?"

"No."

"Why not? You're invited and all 'the girls' will be hoping to see you." Andres laughed.

"We may all be dead before Christmas." Gambrelli lit a cigarette.

They drove a few miles in silence. Then a smile spread across Andres's mouth. "You know, Chief, I've never noticed that Commissioner DeMartell has a 'mischievous twinkle' in his eyes."

"Drive the car, Sergeant, and be quiet. I am thinking."

FOURTEEN

The Rinaldi Theatre dominated the center of the city block on which it had been erected fifty years earlier. Originally built as an opera house, it had become the City's premier location for dramatic plays and Shakespearian festivals in the last ten years. A stone rotunda served as the entrance, and the portico extended far enough onto the sidewalk to make it a haven for shoppers and street urchins during inclement weather. Contrary to the tradition adhered to in other venues the plays of Shakespeare at the Rinaldi were not presented in the spring or summer, but rather in the fall. For this reason, Jean Louis Tremont, an acclaimed Macbeth, Shylock, and Hamlet, occupied the largest dressing room along the rear corridor of the theatre during the months of September and October.

"I'm afraid that you will have to return later, officers," the theatre's manager insisted. "Mr. Tremont is not to be disturbed."

"This will only take a moment," Gambrelli said as he and Andres continued to move down the poorly lit hall, forcing the manager to walk backwards as he tried to block their advance.

"It is in his contract that during this hour of the afternoon, he is to be provided with complete isolation." The manager stopped and held his ground.

"Isolation for what?" Andres asked.

"For meditation, in preparation for his evening performance."

Gambrelli pressed forward, and the manager began to retreat once more. Gambrelli quickened his pace. The manager dragged his left hand against the corridor wall for balance, but Andres took a firm grasp on the manager's arm and pulled him partially off his feet.

"Get out of the way," Andres growled as Gambrelli knocked on Tremont's dressing room door.

"Go away!" A baritone voice bellowed from within the room.

"Police, Monsieur Tremont. Open the door," Gambrelli said as he turned the knob on the locked door.

"Come back later. I cannot be disturbed."

Gambrelli nodded to Andres, who released his grasp of the manager and, with a quick movement, forced the whole of his muscular weight against the door.

As the door gave way, there was an immediate flurry of activity in the room. Tremont closed his dressing gown, and a young man scrambled to his feet, adjusting a pale blue usher's uniform.

"Sorry to disturb you, Jean Louis," Gambrelli said as he entered the room. "I am Chief Inspector Gambrelli of the Metropolitan Police, and this is Detective Sergeant Andres."

"And I am Jean Louis Tremont. What is the meaning of this intrusion?" The actor adjusted the fabric belt of his robe.

Gambrelli looked at the flustered, red-faced usher and waved his hand in a gesture of dismissal. Instead of moving out of the room immediately, the young man delayed his departure awaiting instruction from Tremont. Sergeant Andres grabbed the usher by the nape of his neck and the seat of his pale blue trousers and tossed him into the hallway knocking the theatre manager off his feet as he flew past.

"Nicely done, gentlemen," Tremont said as he closed the door. "A bit crude, but certainly effective." He gently clasped his hand on Andres's bicep. "Yes, most impressive. Now what is it you want of me?"

"Following your performance last Tuesday, you left the theatre in the company of several women; among them was Julienne Vercel. Do you recall?"

"Certainly I do, Julienne is an old friend. Not to say she is old by any means, but none of us stay young forever. Not even a beauty like Julienne." Tremont laughed as he turned to a dressing table and picked up a cigarette, placed it in his mouth, and turned to Gambrelli. "Light, Chief Inspector?"

"At what time did you leave the theatre that evening?" Gambrelli lit a cigarette of his own before lighting Tremont's.

"Let's see, the performance ended at nine-fifty, then a quick change. I talked to the ladies here for a few minutes, then we went out the stage door, caught a cab. I don't know, let's say ten fifteen. I had a dinner engagement for ten thirty and arrived just on time." Tremont adjusted his gown and sat in a high-back rattan chair. "Julienne is all right, isn't she? Nothing is wrong I hope."

"Julienne is fine. At what restaurant was your dinner?" Gambrelli asked.

"The Grotto. It's on Bancroft right off the Boulevard, less than a mile from here."

"Do you remember meeting one of Julienne's friends, a Madame Adele Bertrand?"

"Yes. Strange woman."

"Strange? In what way?"

"Well, at first she was ever so charming, imploring me to provide a dramatic reading for a charity luncheon. Of course I agreed, not for the charity—who knows what it is—but as a favor to Julienne. Then during the cab ride, this Adele went silent. Right in the middle of a conversation, she turned her head away and never looked at me again. Even when they dropped me at the corner on Bancroft and I kissed them all adieu, she never even took my hand. Very moody, I'd say."

From the theatre, the investigators drove east on the Boulevard until they reached Bancroft, where Adele Bertrand's taxi had deposited Tremont.

"Make the run from the theatre again," Gambrelli said, glancing from the sidewalk to his pocket watch and back again. "Once more, only this time, find a taxi heading east and stay behind it."

The sergeant followed the instructions, this time refusing to give in to the impulse of inquiring as to what the significance of the assignment might be.

FIFTEEN

Gambrelli paced about his office, stopping only to poke the coals in the iron stove behind his desk. He rubbed his hands in the narrow halo of warmth the stove provided.

"Madame Gaston," he called to his secretary in the adjoining office, "has Detective Gavros called yet?"

"No, Chief Inspector, not in the two minutes since you last asked," she said in a tone that gave fair enough warning for him not to bother her.

Gambrelli turned on the desk lamp and shuffled through a file that was sitting in the center of the green blotter. He read the same report twice before realizing he could not concentrate. Again, he poked the embers in the coal stove. He looked out his third-story window across the Sôane at the city's Vieux Ville, the Old Town District. The bridges across the river were crowded with early evening traffic, and the café lights lining river's west bank were beginning to glow in the lavender of the encroaching twilight.

He turned from the window, passed through Madame Gaston's office, and entered the large room that housed the detectives of the Major Crimes Bureau. The iron stoves in the detectives' room were not burning. Gambrelli felt a shiver in his back. The room was too cold.

In the far corner of the office, Inspector Robert Renard, elegant in his usual sartorial splendor, sat at his desk next to one of the inactive stoves. Behind him, hanging at a slight angle, was a poster advertising one of the most infamous dance halls and gambling dens in town. The bright colors of the poster made the once-white walls, now yellowed from the smoke of wood, coal, and tobacco, seem even more neglected.

Renard was the same age as Gambrelli and had entered the Major Crimes Bureau more than a decade ago. Considered one of the old-timers like Gambrelli, he was allowed to retain the title of "inspector," a title they all knew would soon be eliminated by the Metropolitan Police reorganization plan that was slowly being implemented by the new breed of police managers. The leader of the reformers was the chief superintendent of investigations, Kirk Wilhelm. Gambrelli couldn't share a room with Wilhelm for more than five minutes without an argument.

"Renard, where is Detective Bruno?" Gambrelli asked.

"He's at the Blue Parrot doing some follow-up interviews with the musicians. One of their dancers was found hacked up last night," Renard said without looking up from his newspaper. "The file is on your desk."

"Yes, I was just looking at it," Gambrelli said.

"Chief Superintendent Wilhelm was searching for you earlier." Renard tossed the paper on his desk and leaned back in his chair, straightening his vest and tie. He ran a comb through his gray hair and moustache. He looked at Gambrelli, then at the other detectives, all of them waiting for their boss's reaction to the mention of Wilhelm's name.

"Let him keep looking for me. It's the only investigation he's capable of," Gambrelli said, not wanting to disappoint his men.

"Narcotics located a photo..." Renard said, "...of a Philippe Gandone... It's five years old. I'll pick it up and show it to the woman at the Savage Gallery. They're putting together what they know about him and will deliver their notes to me later."

"Good," Gambrelli said. "Later tonight you will need a car and Detective Bruno. I want you to drop him off at Central Station a little before ten. Tell him to mix in with the passengers arriving on the last train from Marseilles, then come out with the crowd and walk east on the Boulevard as far as Bancroft and wait there for you to pick him up."

Inspector Renard nodded.

Gambrelli continued. "Once you've dropped him off at the station, take the car to the front of the

Rinaldi Theatre. Wait there until ten-fifteen, then
start driving east with the flow of traffic. Take note
of when and where you overtake Bruno."

"If I see him before Bancroft, should I pull over
and pick him up, or do you want him to walk all the
way regardless?" Renard grinned.

"Do as you like."

Gambrelli returned to his office. He started to
look again at the file of the mutilated dancer, then
jumped up and returned to the detectives' room. He
caught Renard's arm as the inspector was headed
out the door.

"Check with your friends in the Vice Bureau.
Ask them about this Philippe; show them the photograph from the narcotics file. He is a businessman…
his office is probably in the Harbor District, and he
has a taste for women that may run toward vio-
lence. Tell them to ask around. Maybe he's roughed
up a professional girl or two."

Gambrelli returned to his office and closed the
files he hadn't the patience to read. From his desk
drawer, he took a Berretta pistol and slid it into his
waistband. He struggled with his damp overcoat as
he passed his secretary's desk.

"I'm going out. Call me at the Ship's Tavern
when you hear from Gavros."

Halfway through a bowl of cabbage soup,
Gambrelli lost interest. Flipping the pages of his
notebook, he searched for anything that might have
escaped his attention. Finally, he set the book down

and looked through the small panes of the tavern windows. The rain had stopped.

He watched the slow-moving barge traffic along the Saône. Tarpaulins of dark green and black covered the merchandise on its way to the harbor to be off-loaded onto merchant ships, bound for who knew where. The barges carried the products of rural labor. Some were laden with barrels of wine, some with produce from the farms outside the city, probably from farms not far from the Vercel estate. He laughed to himself and rubbed his gray head at the thought of Julienne Vercel and her memories—his memories as well.

He took the phone from behind the bar and kindly asked the operator to connect him to his residence. The voice of Marie Gambrelli on the other end of the line warmed him.

"Yes, I'm back in town."

"Did your trip go well?"

"Who can say?"

"Will you be home for dinner? The girls are coming."

"No. I will be late."

"I'm making beef bourguignon the way you like it, à l'ancienne."

Gambrelli hesitated. He thought he could taste the dish.

"Well, no matter," Marie Gambrelli said. "It will keep no matter how late."

"Don't worry I've just had some soup."

"And several beers, I would guess."

"Only one."

"By the way, your friend Odin slept on your side of the bed last night."

"Because he missed me, or does he think he's taking over?"

"You'll have to ask him. It was actually quite pleasant; he doesn't snore."

"He most certainly does."

"We received a letter from your sister today. The rain is pushing the grape harvest up. She said if it doesn't dry out in the next few days, you may have to realign your vacation to accommodate an early harvest; that is, if we're going to help."

"And her husband is he too busy to be of use?"

"Now Artu, be kind. It serves no use to excite yourself. She also said that the Clouet vineyards may be for sale."

"I can't count how many times over the last hundred years the Gambrelli family has tried to buy land from the Clouets. It's no use."

"She said she talked to the grandson, he's a lawyer in Montluçon, and he is willing to discuss the sale of a portion of the property. It is the hillside across the creek. Your sister said you would know what she is talking about. She said it's the hill you always wanted to expand the Grenache and add more Syrah vines."

"I know it. We'll see if he really wants to sell." Gambrelli watched Sergeant Andres pass in front of the tavern and reach for the door. "Marie, I have to go. I will be home as soon as I can. Give the girls my love."

"Oh, wait, I wanted to tell you about Odin... at the park yesterday..." She stopped as if sensing she had already lost his attention. "Never mind, it can wait... besides I'd rather tell you in person."

Andres signaled to the bartender for a beer. "Chief, we just got a call from Gavros. He's at the girl's apartment on Leopold Street."

"Is she there?"

"No, she moved out."

"When?"

"Last week, late Tuesday night or early Wednesday morning." Andres raised the cold glass to his lips.

"Did she leave a forwarding address?"

"Gavros said the concierge didn't have one."

"Leave the beer. We have no time to waste."

SIXTEEN

Even in the dark, Gambrelli noted the refinement of the apartment house on Leopold Street. It was one of those well-maintained buildings that kept a discrete distance from the passing traffic. Separated from the street by a neatly trimmed lawn, several large trees, and strategically placed rows of boxwoods, it conveyed a feeling of gentility.

The entrance was wide. Gambrelli and Andres were almost able to pass through side by side. The black front door had the faint smell of having been recently painted in preparation for the approaching winds of winter.

The apartment house concierge was waiting in the foyer for their arrival. The portly man was probably close to seventy. His white shirt, starched and buttoned at the neck pinched his pink skin. His black vest was unbuttoned and most likely hadn't enough material to conceal his girth for several years. He shifted his weight from one heavy leg to the other as if trying to balance his protruding stomach. He extended a hand to greet the new arrivals.

"Chief Inspector, an honor. This way." The concierge turned to the elevator.

In his haste, Gambrelli had chosen to forgo the stairs, a decision he immediately regretted. He forced himself to focus on the receding black-and-white, tiles of the apartment house lobby as the birdcage lift groaned upward. The circular main staircase of the building curved around their ascending line. He did not like confined spaces, and the slow movement of the cage, straining against the weight of its occupants, made him uncomfortable. He began to sweat under his damp overcoat. He estimated the cage was designed to accommodate two persons of average size, so Gambrelli was certain they were demanding performance beyond the lift's ability to deliver. The corpulent concierge pressed against his left arm and the bulk of Sergeant Andres was against his right.

Gambrelli controlled his breathing to dispel his growing fear that the grinding cable would snap, sending the trio into the basement below. None of the three occupants were speaking. Maybe, he thought, they were all contemplating the precariousness of their mutual suspension.

The mechanism hauling the cage upward ground to a stop, then shuddered and suddenly dropped an inch to align the lift's metal floor with the fourth level of the building. Gambrelli swung open the ornate metal gate and rushed onto the landing. A few paces later, he was breathing again.

Detective Peter Gavros was standing in the doorway of an apartment down the hall to the right of the lift. "Over here, Chief," Gavros called to Gambrelli, who was still regaining his composure.

Gambrelli gave a quick glance to Sergeant Andres as a signal to keep the concierge in the hall and out of the way, and then followed Gavros into the apartment.

Detective Gavros attempted to lead Gambrelli through the small apartment as if assuming the role of a real estate agent. They entered directly from the hall into the living room. To the left of the door, against the far wall, was a battered couch covered in a thin burgundy fabric with a tattered fringe that unevenly touched against the wooden floor. Behind the couch was a large window. Gambrelli moved to the window, noting it overlooked the street passing in front of the building. The streetlamp below cast weak shadows on the doorways of the two buildings across the street and the mouth of the alley between them.

"The kitchen is here on the left, and the bedroom and bath are to your right," Gavros said.

"Really? Thank you, Detective," Gambrelli said dryly. "I never would have guessed." He lit a cigarette. "Is there anything of interest you have discovered while familiarizing yourself with the floor plan?"

The tone of the chief inspector's voice was enough to send Gavros back to the apartment door without reply.

From the center of the living room, Gambrelli looked through the archway into the bedroom where, until a few days ago, Lisa Cuomo had slept. In five strides, he was standing between two small beds. He sat on the corner of the bed nearest the window; the springs creaked under his weight.

He looked around the room and saw a wooden dresser and an armoire with mirrored doors on his left, the window to his right. Between the window and archway sat a Queen Anne chair and a small round table that held the room's only lamp. The bedroom window provided an unobstructed view of the brick wall of the neighboring building not more than ten feet away.

He turned on the table lamp and used its minimal light to probe the dresser and armoire. Nothing, not even a pin, was left behind. The bathroom was small, but in older buildings in the University District, it was an extravagant amenity. The apartment, aside from its worn-out furniture and scuffed wooden floors, held no indication that anyone had recently lived in it. Lisa Cuomo was gone. Would they be able to find her in time was Gambrelli's only concern as he looked at the tiny bed.

"They were here earlier, about an hour before Detective Gavros," the concierge said to Sergeant Andres.

"Who was this?" Gambrelli joined the men in the hall.

"Two men," Andres said. "Looking for the girl."

"Did they ask for her by name?" Gambrelli asked.

"Yes, but when I told them she had moved and I couldn't tell them where, they asked if her apartment was for rent. I told them it had been cleaned and was ready today, if they were interested. They asked to see it, so I brought them up here, just like you." The concierge looked at Gambrelli, then averted his eyes, appearing unsure if he should be proud of the information he was supplying, or if he would soon be in trouble with the police.

Gambrelli looked at Detective Gavros with a stare and the locking of his jaw that often prefaced the chief inspector's rage.

"I called it in, with the descriptions of the men. Bruno took the message," Gavros offered as a preemptive defense.

Gambrelli nodded, indicating that the moment was defused.

"Have you ever seen these men before?" Gambrelli asked.

"No, never." The concierge appeared certain. "My wife would be a better one to ask. She is always attending the front of the building."

"Where is she?"

"Gone to her sister's for a few days. She will be back tomorrow."

"When she gets back, describe the men to her. Then call me at Police Headquarters and let me know what she has to say."

"As soon as she returns, I will do it," the concierge said eagerly.

"And you were with these men when they looked around the apartment?" Gambrelli asked. "You watched them?"

"Well, not exactly. I opened the door for them, and then the larger fellow asked me a lot of questions about the leasing agreement while the small gent looked the place over. Just like your men did to me now, keeping me busy while you poked around."

"Did they say anything else?"

"No, I don't recall ..."

"Think," Gambrelli pushed.

"The one with the beard asked where the closet was." The concierge brightened at the recollection. "I told him there was no closet, only the armoire in the bedroom."

"And when they were done looking over the apartment, they left?" Gambrelli asked.

"Straight away. We went back to the lift and ..." The concierge paused and rubbed a swollen hand against the back of his thick neck. He looked up at Gambrelli. "Before we went down, the taller one said he must have dropped his pen in the hall. He left me in the lift with the shorter one for a few minutes. He came back with the pen in his hand and said it had been right outside the apartment door. I'm not sure, but I thought I heard him jingling keys and trying to get a key in the lock. I could be wrong, but I thought I heard it."

"Did you hear the door open?"

"No, just the scratching of the key against the lock, not the sound of it going in. It was like he had the wrong keys and wasn't able to get them to fit."

"Did Lisa Cuomo leave anything behind?" Gambrelli asked.

"A few old books and some photographs."

"And where are these items now?"

"I put them in a box and stored them in the basement. All the tenants know whatever they leave behind is stored for thirty days; after that, I toss it out or sell it. It's perfectly legal." The concierge looked at each policeman in turn as if to assure himself they were satisfied with the protection the law provided to a landlord exercising his discretion.

"Sergeant Andres, accompany our friend to the storage room and bring back the box." Gambrelli stepped back into the apartment with Detective Gavros and closed the door.

"I did not get your message; describe the two men to me," Gambrelli said to Gavros, who quickly pulled a notebook from his jacket pocket and began reading aloud.

"Both were in their late thirties. The taller man may be a little older, he was bald, or at least appeared so. The concierge said he was 'ugly,' scars on his face, a twisted nose, thick lips, and possibly missing teeth. He wore a black, knit seaman's cap, black jacket, and dark pants. He was thin, 'almost like a skeleton.'"

Gavros looked at Gambrelli, who lit another cigarette and nodded that the detective should continue.

"The shorter man had dark hair and a full beard, and was also wearing dark clothing. He was stocky, five foot seven, eighty-six kilos, give or take. He was wearing heavy work boots. The concierge said the boot leather creaked when he walked."

Gambrelli moved about the apartment, opening and closing cupboards and giving no indication to Gavros as to whether he was listening or not. He was sitting on the edge of the bed nearest the window when Andres and the concierge returned with the box and set it on the narrow kitchen counter.

The contents of the box were as the concierge had described. There were three well-worn books: one contained reproductions of renaissance art, the other two were textbooks on anatomy. There were two photographs in wooden frames: the larger featured the two sisters standing side by side amid adult relatives, and the smaller had the two girls sitting on the steps of a country church.

"Do you know where Lisa Cuomo worked?" Gambrelli asked.

"That's what the two others asked me, and I'll tell you the same as I told them; some bookstore over by the university, not far, because she walked to work." The concierge picked up the photograph of the girls in front of the church. "The older one is her sister, Annette. Pretty girls, aren't they? Almost like twins. And proper too; no noise, no mess, no men coming and going. Though she quit the place without advanced notice, she was kind enough to leave two weeks' rent in an envelope."

Gambrelli picked up one of the anatomy books and leafed through the pages. Then he set the book on the counter, his finger pointing to a bluish, stamped marking on the frontispiece.

"C and D, Portia Street," Gambrelli read. He checked the other books. Each had the same mark. "Do you know a 'C and D' bookseller on Portia Street?" he asked the three men, who returned his question with a combination of blank stares and shaking heads.

He grabbed the concierge's arm.

"Where is your phone?"

"There is one in the vestibule, to the right of the entrance." He rubbed his arm where Gambrelli had squeezed it. "There was another man who was looking for Annette."

"When?" Gambrelli asked.

"One day last week, I'm not sure which. He spoke to my wife."

"Was it one of the men you saw earlier today?"

"I don't think so. My wife said he was well-dressed and good-looking. That doesn't fit the two that were here today."

"I will need to speak to your wife tomorrow, without fail."

Gambrelli left the apartment and descended the curving staircase, leaving the others to determine who should carry the box. Gavros, also having taken the stairs, was the first to join the chief inspector in the lobby while Andres and the concierge descended in the lift.

Gambrelli was on the phone waiting for the police operator to connect him to the Major Crimes Bureau when Gavros appeared at his side. Gambrelli cupped his hand over the mouthpiece of the receiver and addressed the young detective.

"Do you have your gun?"

"It's in my desk."

Gambrelli turned his attention to the phone. "Lanier, this is Gambrelli. Get a car and pick up Gavros at twenty-seven Leopold Street. And get Gavros's gun from his desk…Yes now… He will fill you in when you arrive. Be quick."

Sergeant Andres and the concierge emerged from the lift. The sergeant was carrying the box containing Lisa Cuomo's belongings and trailing behind his waddling companion.

Gambrelli pulled Gavros toward the entry door. "You and Lanier find that bookstore. When you get your hands on the girl, keep her safe and call me at once." He took a photograph from his inside coat pocket and handed it to Gavros. "This is a recent picture of Lisa. I removed it from her sister's home. Make sure Lanier gets a good look at it." He pulled the young detective further aside. "And never leave your gun behind again; you're in the Major Crimes Bureau now, lad."

He left Gavros standing in the lobby as he called to Andres.

"Sergeant, leave the box. Quickly, to the car."

.   .   .

The rain had stopped and was replaced by a fog and mist the headlights barely penetrated.

"Drive to Prosecutor Bertrand's home," Gambrelli said.

"What do you make of it, Chief?" Andres asked.

"I don't know."

"Do you think the two men are Annette Cuomo's killers?"

"We must consider that a strong possibility."

The two investigators rode in silence for several minutes before Gambrelli began to think out loud.

"Annette's gallery on the island was losing money. Her sister, Lisa, couldn't have been earning more than a few francs at a used bookstore. Yet Annette was seen with several thousand francs in cash when she returned to the island from the City last Wednesday, and announced her plans to expand her business. At the same time, Lisa was able to pay a few weeks' rent in advance—in cash." Gambrelli lit two cigarettes, handing one to Andres.

"So sometime Tuesday night, they hit it rich," Andres offered.

"Exactly, and before Wednesday morning, Lisa moves, flees in the middle of the night, leaving no forwarding address. A few days later, Annette has a new lock installed on her door, changes her plans, and tells Bertrand, a man to whom she had been devoted, to get out of her life.

"Later that night, she is murdered, and two days after that, there are a couple of roughnecks trying to hunt down Lisa."

Andres abruptly swerved the car, narrowly missing a woman standing in the road. "They stole from the wrong crowd if you ask me." He settled the car in the center of the boulevard and pressed the accelerator.

SEVENTEEN

The Bertrand home was one of several stately residences that lined a fashionable street in the south end of the city's central district. Gas lamps on either side of the large, ebony entry doors illuminated Gambrelli's identity card as he presented it to the young woman who answered his knock.

"Police. We are here to speak with Adele Bertrand."

"Are you expected?"

"We are rarely expected, Mademoiselle."

"Madame Bertrand cannot be disturbed at the moment." The young woman stood her ground.

"Fetch your mistress, or I will find her myself."

"I told you she cannot—"

Gambrelli and Andres pushed past her and entered the house. Gambrelli turned a cold expression to the young woman, who was still standing in the open doorway.

"Please tell Madame Bertrand we are waiting."

Uninvited, Gambrelli walked from the entry hall into the drawing room. He threw his damp coat over the back of a finely upholstered chair and immediately began inspecting the photographs displayed along the mantelpiece above the burning fireplace. The photographs were set at slight angles radiating from the center of the mantel. Each picture was presented in silver-and-gold frames of deco design. None of the photos pictured Jean Michel and Adele Bertrand together; instead, every photograph showed them separately with well-known public figures, all in formal attire, looking artificially amused.

Gambrelli thought of Lisa Cuomo's photographs in their simple wooden frames. How truly happy the girls had looked. How their comfort in each other's company showed in their faces. He also observed that in none of the photographs on the mantel did the prosecutor look as alive as he had in the snap shot standing next to Annette Cuomo. It was something in his eyes.

"Chief Inspector Gambrelli?" Adele Bertrand's voice betrayed no hint of hostility at the unexpected intrusion into her home. She was tall and thin, wearing a black evening dress that Gambrelli thought revealed a bit too much of her bony chest. She carried a dark satin coat over her left arm in a manner that indicated she was planning to leave immediately. She extended a sinewy hand.

"My husband has mentioned you often, although, I must confess, not always in the most flattering of terms." She smiled the practiced smile of one accustomed to being gracious during unpleasant encounters.

"This is Detective Sergeant Andres. We would like—"

"I'm afraid my husband is not at home. He is out of town on Ministry business and is not expected to return until tomorrow." Adele Bertrand moved toward the door, as if to indicate that the meeting was over and it was time for the intruders to leave.

"We are here to talk to you, not your husband," Gambrelli said, as Andres stepped in front of her.

"Actually, I was just about to go out. I'm running a bit late for a dinner party at the deputy mayor's home, his thirty-year-wedding anniversary." She paused apparently waiting for the importance of her social obligation to dawn on the men blocking her exit. "Might we make an arrangement to talk tomorrow? I'm free all afternoon." She turned to consult an appointment book sitting on the corner of a carved Louis XIV-style desk near the window.

Gambrelli waited until her hand was on the book, then he lit a cigarette. At the sound of his lighter, she gave him a stern look.

"I would prefer you not smoke in my house, Chief Inspector."

He pointed around the room.

"Are all these ashtrays merely for decoration?"

"They are for my husband and our invited guests. Since you are neither, I would prefer you refrain from smoking."

"And I would prefer to be at home, having dinner with my wife and daughters." He exhaled a cloud of smoke in her direction. "Your husband has been arrested by the provincial police," he said in a quiet but firm tone.

He waited. Her hand hovered above the appointment book before she turned to face him. He studied her. For a moment she appeared to be staggered by his words, like a fighter caught by an unexpected blow to the solar plexus. But like a fighter prepared for combat, she recovered quickly and went on the offensive.

"Arrested? There must be some mistake. My husband is the senior prosecutor of the Ministry of Justice. Surely you are—"

"I assure you, Madame, there is no mistake."

"And what is the charge?" She advanced on Gambrelli, closing the distance as if fearless of his power.

"A young woman was murdered on the Island of Q. Your husband has been charged with the crime." Again she was taken by surprise, the strength drained from her legs, but this time Gambrelli did not wait for her to recover. "The victim's name is Annette Cuomo. I believe you know her."

"Annette Cuomo ..." She repeated the name as if searching her memory for a connection to her life. "No, I don't believe—"

"Madame Bertrand." Gambrelli's voice was now hard. "I am not part of your social circle. I do not contribute to your charities. I am a policeman with very little time to waste and absolutely no interest in charades." He watched her arms begin to fall to her sides. "Now, we have some questions—"

"I have nothing to say to you. I will not be interrogated like a common criminal." She temporarily regained her composure. "Need I remind you to whom you are speaking?"

"I'm well aware of who you are. I must now determine what you are." He paused to let her process the fact that he was not going to offer her any quarter. "Now since you will not cooperate I must insist—"

"Who are you to insist anything in my home?"

He turned and walked two steps away from her. He needed a moment to let the image of her snarling lips drain from his mind. As the tension in his shoulders subsided he turned back.

"You will accompany the detective sergeant to Police Headquarters and await my arrival. When we meet there, you will provide full and complete answers to my questions. You will need to make your statements as accurate as you can."

"Are you arresting me?"

"I would prefer to think that you are voluntarily assisting the police in our investigation." He took another drag from the cigarette, allowing the smoke to escape with his words. "However, if you waste another minute of my time, you will be handcuffed, thrown into the back of the car, and locked away in the darkest cell I can find."

She was done. Whatever she may have thought she could hurl at the chief inspector to stop his advance she abandoned.

"Now, go," he said with a wave of the back of his hand as he dismissed her from his presence.

Sergeant Andres helped Adele Bertrand into her coat, pulling the fabric gently over her lifeless arms. He then took her by her right elbow and escorted her to the door. She stopped in the doorway, straightened herself, and looked toward Gambrelli.

"My husband is right. You are a vicious bastard."

"Prepare to confess Madame Bertrand. I'll be along in a little while." He crossed the room and threw his cigarette into the fire. Through a partially open window he heard the door of the police car slam shut, the engine start up, and drive away.

Although he did not feel like smoking he lit another cigarette. Perhaps it was a need to thumb his nose at Madame Bertrand. Maybe he was becoming more spiteful in his old age. Perhaps he had always been this way. He couldn't decide.

The confrontation with Adele Bertrand did not go well. On the way to her home he had decided to play a heavy hand, to shake her from her comfortable perch. Had she refused to leave he would have had to retreat. There was not a judge in all of France who would have authorized his request for an arrest warrant. There was no evidence to link her to the murder of the Cuomo woman. He had nothing. Nothing but a desire to know whatever truth there was to this whole affair.

The weight of his situation made him feel exhausted. He sat on the arm of the sofa. At that moment he couldn't explain to himself just what was he doing. Suddenly he was seized with a fear that all this rushing around the city, dispatching his detectives as if he was on the trail of a solution was just a fool's errand.

He slid onto the sofa. There was a time, not so long ago, that he would have thundered through the streets shaking the foundations of the city confident in his every gesture: a knight on a quest to vanquish the forces of evil. Now he was tired. He seemed to be losing his way. Several times in the last year, alone on the street, he heard himself ask; *Who cares?*

He had no case, of any sort. The only prosecutable case was against Bertrand. Beyond that there was no case, just a feeling that there was an answer to be found in the city. Even if he found one, it would be for an investigation being conducted by Major Ormond. In the strictest sense this was of no official concern to the Metropolitan Police. Yet he was putting himself at risk. A complaint regarding his conduct, placed with Chief Superintendent Wilhelm, by Madame Bertrand and her lawyers would bring the roof down, and provide Wilhelm with the justification, he so often sought, to demand his replacement as the head of the Major Crime Bureau.

Well it was too late now. The hand had been played. He would have a second turn when he met with her again at headquarters.

He inspected the appointment book on the carved desk. A phone number was written on the space designated for the previous Wednesday. From his pocket, he pulled the one-hundred-franc note he had taken from the Savage Gallery. Scrawled on the top of the note was the same number Adele Bertrand had written in her appointment book.

EIGHTEEN

For seventy-five years the three front windows of the Watchman's Tavern, opening onto Cours de la Liberté, had provided an unobstructed view of the entrance to the Préfecture de Police. For all that time the tavern had served as a gathering place for policemen of all rank, either at the beginning or end of their shift. As a result, it was most crowded at six in the morning, two in the afternoon, and ten at night.

The ownership of the tavern changed about every ten years, passing from one retired police sergeant to another. It seemed to Gambrelli their only qualifications for ownership were having been loved and respected by the officers they had worked with, and having the uncanny ability to hire the prettiest, most buxom and foul-mouthed waitresses the city had to offer.

Gambrelli looked at his watch. It was twenty minutes past ten. The tavern was full of faces he

recognized, and many had names he could still remember. His infrequent presence in the tavern was
often cause for rounds of nostalgic remembrances
by the senior officers lamenting the passing of the
"good old days" when policing was not a job for
the faint of heart.

On the occasions when he stopped in for a quick
drink with the men, he would sit at the end of the
zinc bar with his back to the windows. However,
tonight he sat at a small café table looking out the
center window at the oversized brass doors of Police Headquarters. He monitored the comings and
goings with uncharacteristic intensity. His mood
was somber. No one lingered at his table longer
than to offer a brief hello, or to deliver a clap on the
back. Gambrelli had something on his mind, and
the street-smart policemen knew to leave the chief
inspector alone.

He was sipping his second cup of coffee when
a detective's car drove through the entry gates of
the Prefecture. Gambrelli recognized the lanky,
gray-haired detective in a stylish, French-cut suit
bounding up the steps to the entry doors. Inspector
Renard and Detective Bruno were back from the
theatre.

Moments later, Gambrelli came through the
entrance to headquarters and nodded to the desk
sergeant, who peered over the standard pile of paperwork that never diminished. Renard and Bruno
were waiting for the lift when they saw their boss
enter the mosaic-tiled lobby. They slowly walked

toward the stairs, neither looking too pleased that now they would have to climb the three flights to the offices of the Major Crimes Bureau.

"It was just like clockwork, Patron," Renard spoke as Gambrelli moved the files from the center of his desk. "I left the theatre after the rush, like you said, and headed east on the Boulevard. Just as I passed the train station, I spotted Detective Bruno in the crowd moving down the sidewalk. I pulled over at the next corner and picked him up and we came right back here."

"Excellent." Gambrelli picked up the last file under which he found Gavros' message containing the concierge's description of the two men that had been looking for Lisa Cuomo. He folded the message and placed it in his coat pocket. "Did your contacts in the Vice Bureau have any information on this Philippe character?"

"No," Renard said. "But the boys in narcotics came up with more information. They knew a Philippe Gandone, a produce importer with a warehouse in the Harbor District, who matches the general description." He handed Gambrelli a photograph. "This is the booking photo of Gandone. I showed it to the manager of the Savage Gallery. She identified him as the man looking for Annette Cuomo. He was arrested five years ago. The file listed him as the owner of a transport vessel, the Black Swan. It was seized by the Coastal Patrol for carrying opium hidden under boxes of pears."

"Did he go to prison?" Gambrelli asked.

"No, but the captain of the Black Swan and the five-man crew did." Inspector Renard consulted his notes. "The captain got eight years; he's still in. The others did three; they're all out."

"And none of them implicated Gandone?" Gambrelli studied the booking photo.

"Not a word. Lieutenant Vigier handled the case when he was a sergeant. His informants said that Gandone bought the crew's silence by agreeing to make monthly payments to the wives of the married men and to hold a similar allotment for the others to be collected when they got out."

Gambrelli picked up his desk phone and told the switchboard operator to connect him to the Narcotics Bureau. He set the photograph of Philippe Gandone on his desk.

"Vigier, this is Gambrelli. Do you have a couple of men available to locate Philippe Gandone? ... Good. If they find him, have them keep him under surveillance and call Inspector Renard; he will be here at Major Crimes awaiting their call ... No, I would prefer they take no action until they hear from me ... I'm not certain, but I believe if all goes well this evening, there will be more than enough to justify Gandone's arrest ... That will be up to the courts, but we can at least make the next few days of his life uncomfortable."

Renard and Bruno were headed back to the detectives' bay when Gambrelli hung up the phone.

"Inspector Renard, I want you to wait here. There is a woman I want you to obtain a statement from." He looked at Detective Michael Bruno. "She is in interrogation room four. Bring her to me."

Gambrelli completed cleaning off the top of his desk by stacking all the paperwork and shoving it into the bottom drawer. He then moved the extra chairs against the walls, creating a large, open space in front of his desk. He motioned to Renard to stand along the wall next to one of the empty chairs. He checked a ceramic pitcher to be sure it contained cool water and set it next to three glasses on a narrow pine table. From a file cabinet, he removed a thick file and placed it on the edge of his desk. On the outside cover, he wrote in large letters:

Homicide: Annette CUOMO

He sat behind his desk and placed the photograph of Philippe Gandone inside the file. From the desk drawer, he took another file and casually flipped through its pages. He looked up at Inspector Renard, who was leaning on the wall, appearing completely comfortable with the role he was to perform in the familiar scenario that was about to unfold.

A few minutes later, Detective Bruno entered Gambrelli's office, a firm grip on Adele Bertrand's left arm. Bruno maneuvered her to the open area in front of the desk, released his grip, and retreated, leaving the woman standing before the chief inspector. In the silence uncertainty was allowed to grow in Madame Bertrand's imagination. Gambrelli did not acknowledge the woman's arrival. Nor was she offered the courtesy of a chair.

After a measured wait, Gambrelli closed the file and looked up at Adele Bertrand. It was obvious that she had been crying. Her figure now appeared more frail than fashionable, almost pathetic, Gambrelli thought.

"Are you ready to make a statement?"

"I don't know what you want me to say."

"The truth!" He slammed a flattened palm against the top of the desk. "All we are interested in is the truth."

"I'm...I'm not sure ..." she stammered.

"Oh, but I believe you are quite sure, Madame. Quite sure Annette Cuomo lies dead in the morgue on the Island of Q. Sure your husband is to be charged with her murder—a murder he did not commit, but in which you played a role. And if you do not tell me every detail, I will see to it that you are charged in this matter."

Adele Bertrand lost her strength. Her legs could no longer hold. Inspector Renard moved with the grace of a dancer crossing the room, sliding a chair under the collapsing woman while gently guiding her downward. Once seated, she touched Renard's forearm as a gesture of gratitude. He remained by her side as Gambrelli came out from behind the desk, pulled another chair close to hers. He sat facing her, their knees a few centimeters apart. She stiffened at his proximity.

"Madame Bertrand," Gambrelli began, keeping his voice low and quiet. "I know this is difficult for you. Let me tell you what I believe. If I am mistaken, correct me. Do you understand?"

She nodded, but did not raise her eyes to meet his.

"You and Jean Michel have been married for over twenty years. During that time, you have incrementally drifted apart. He was consumed by his work at the Ministry and the management of his investments, and you by your social obligations and charitable works.

"Your life was nonetheless more than comfortable. Each of you had substantial means, and together, your wealth rose to what would be considered, by any standard, as a considerable fortune. Additionally, Jean Michel's ancestry provided a connection to the aristocracy, which allowed you access to circles from which you would otherwise have been excluded, regardless of your wealth. And you used those connections for the benefit of the charitable causes you hold so dear.

"Then on Saturday night, the twenty-fifth of August, while at the University Club, you noticed on the reservation register that Jean Michel had entertained Charles Goddard at lunch the previous day. The name Goddard was not unknown to you as he has been instrumental in the dissolution of several marriages within your circle of acquaintances. Maybe it was then you began to consider the possibility that Jean Michel was thinking of leaving you."

Adele Bertrand began to cry, and Inspector Renard placed a crisply pressed handkerchief in her hand. She looked up at him. "Thank you," she said and raised the cloth to her eyes.

Gambrelli waited for her to regain a modicum of composure before he began again.

"Three nights later, Tuesday the twenty-eighth, you and your companions left the Rinaldi Theatre in the company of the actor Jean Louis Tremont. Your taxi passed in front of Central Station just as the late-night travelers from the coastal train were pouring on to the boulevard.

There, amid the crowd, you saw your husband, but he was not alone. He was in the arms of a beautiful young woman. A woman you immediately recognized as Annette Cuomo, the art broker from the Savage Gallery, with whom you have spent many hours.

"Instantly, many things made sense to you: your husband's investment in an art shop and cottage on the Island of Q, his new responsibility requiring his travel to the island almost weekly on Ministry business, his luncheon with the divorce attorney, Goddard. Possibly you considered his uncharacteristic contentment. What other conclusion could a woman come to? Jean Michel was planning on leaving you. Life as you knew it was about to end."

She started to cry again. Gambrelli looked at Renard, who nodded his concurrence that all was going well. Renard then poured a glass of water from the ceramic pitcher and returned to Adele Bertrand's side, handing her the glass when her tears subsided. She raised the glass to her lips with a shaking hand, took several sips, and then held the glass until Renard took it from her.

"But you were not going down without a fight." Gambrelli quickened the pace of his narrative. "You went to the Savage Gallery the following morning to confront your rival. Instead, you learned she had moved away. A man, a violent man, was also there to find Annette. But no one could tell him where she had gone. However, you knew where she had gone: to the Island of Q, where she lived in a cottage by the sea and operated a small shop on the town's main street. A cottage and a shop you had seen months earlier; a cottage and shop purchased by your husband for Annette Cuomo."

"No, I didn't."

"And so, when the man stormed out of the gallery, you followed him. Possibly thinking that he was Annette's former lover, you caught up with him at the corner and told him what you knew of her location, hoping he might seek her out and drive Jean Michel from her life." He leaned toward Adele. "Have I missed anything?"

"I did not tell him about the island. I was not sure. I hadn't even begun to put the pieces together."

Gambrelli was momentarily stunned. He had not expected Adele Bertrand to deny telling Gandone about Annette's location. If she had not told

Gandone, then who had supplied that important piece of information? He stopped himself from exploring that thought.

"Then what did you tell him?"

"That I was looking for her as well. That my husband worked for the Ministry of Justice and might be able to find her."

"Did he ask why you were looking for her?"

"I told him it was a matter concerning a painting I had purchased. He gave me his phone number and asked me to call him if I found out anything."

"And did you call him? Did you give him Annette Cuomo's location?"

She shook her head. "No." She looked Gambrelli in the eyes for the first time. "She was shameless. I had seen her on two occasions walking past our home, peering at the windows. One morning, I watched her stand across the street for at least thirty minutes pretending to busy herself with a flower vendor."

"When was this?" Gambrelli asked.

"In the last month."

"Did you tell your husband?"

"I did. He insisted I was mistaken."

"Could you have been?"

"Possibly... I don't know... I don't know anything anymore." She began to cry into Inspector Renard's handkerchief.

Gambrelli opened the file on the corner of the desk, took out the booking photo of Philippe Gandone, and showed it to her. "Is this the man you followed from the gallery?"

"Yes."

"And what is his name?"

"Philippe."

"Philippe what?"

"Philippe is all I know."

Gambrelli stood up and tossed the photo on the desk. "Thank you, Madame Bertrand." He laid a hand on her thin shoulder. "Now you will accompany Inspector Renard to another office where you will prepare a written statement." He addressed Renard. "Start where she observes Gandone at the Savage Gallery. It is only important, at this point, that she accurately details his description, everything she told him, and what she heard him say in reply. And include her identification of his photograph. Anything else can wait until later."

Gambrelli lit a cigarette and poured a glass of brandy from a bottle he kept beneath his desk. Moments later, Inspector Renard returned to the office. Gambrelli glared at him.

"When the statement is made, what do you want to do with her?" Renard asked.

"Take her home. We have no further use for her." Gambrelli sipped the brandy. "And don't leave her alone again until her statement is complete."

Gambrelli placed his feet on top of the desk and took another sip of brandy.

"Chief." Andres stood in the doorway to Gambrelli's office. "Gavros is on the phone. They located the girl."

"Where?"

"A few blocks from North Station."

"Where are they now?" Gambrelli stood up.

"At her apartment." Andres waved a slip of paper in the air. "I've got the address."

Gambrelli set his glass down, hurried into the detectives' bay, and grabbed the phone.

"Talk to me," Gambrelli growled.

"We picked her up a few blocks from North Station. We brought her back to her apartment—her new apartment. Lanier is upstairs with her now. I'm using the phone in the concierge's office. The building is in Vieux Ville...I gave the address—"

"Did you see anyone watching the apartment?"

"No. Not at first."

"But there was someone?"

"As a precaution, I first came into the building alone, leaving her in the car with Lanier."

"Go on."

"On my way up the stairs, I passed a man who matched the description of the stocky, bearded suspect."

"Where is he now?"

"Gone. He went out the front entrance and walked west."

"Did he see the girl?"

"No. Lanier was parked to the east."

Gambrelli took a deep breath and paused for a moment. "Go back to the girl's room. You and Lanier stay on your guard. Do not pass in front of the windows. Secure the door. Allow no one to enter before I get there. Do you understand?"

"Got it."

"If you are right about the man on the stairs, then they already know where she lives and are preparing to confront her. These men have killed before. Take no chances." Gambrelli closed his hand over the receiver. "Andres, get the car. I'll meet you out front." He then spoke into the receiver again. His voice was calm and slow. "I'm on my way. And Gavros, do not trust the lock. They have a key."

NINETEEN

Gambrelli descended the final curve of the wide marble steps that, prior to the construction of the new wing, had served as the entrance to Police Headquarters. Across the tiled lobby, he saw Sergeant Duran and Lieutenant Vigier standing in front of the duty sergeant's desk. On the bench along the wall behind the desk, Gambrelli noticed the young officer who had driven him to the train station the previous morning. He intended to pass them with only a nod when Vigier called his name.

"My men have located Gandone. He is in his office at the produce warehouse."

Gambrelli slowed his stride as Vigier continued.

"I told them to stay on him and keep me updated if he leaves."

Gambrelli paused with his hand on the brass entry door. "Inspector Renard is in the interrogation room on the third floor. Notify him when Gandone moves, and tell him to take Detective Bruno to back

up your men." He then addressed the young officer
sitting on the bench. "Officer Luzon!" The young
officer sat up straight. "Do you know Inspector Renard or Detective Bruno?"

"I know Detective Bruno, sir."

"They will be escorting a woman out of the
building in a few minutes. You will be their driver.
You will remain with them for the rest of the night."
Then to Sergeant Duran he said, "If Superintendent
Wilhelm calls, tell him I have reassigned Officer
Luzon to assist in an urgent police investigation."

Sergeant Duran lit a cigar and turned a great
smile toward Gambrelli. "It will be my pleasure
to inform the superintendent of that fact, Chief
Inspector."

·   ·   ·

After two passes in front of Lisa Cuomo's apartment house, Gambrelli was reasonably sure there
was no one watching the front entrance. As a precaution, Sergeant Andres parked on a side street
three blocks away. To avoid detection they made
their way on foot using *traboules* that linked the
intervening streets. As they navigated the tunnel like
passageways Gambrelli was forced to rely on the
small flame of his cigarette lighter to help him along
the stone path and walls. For the last hundred yards
they had no choice but to use connecting alleyways.
Gambrelli strained his eyes in the dark between the
brick buildings to avoid discarded trash and to keep
his shoes out of the deeper puddles. They entered

the apartment house from the alley and climbed to the fifth floor.

The apartment was smaller than the one recently vacated on Leopold Street. It was made smaller still by the presence of the four investigators and their wet wool coats hovering above Lisa Cuomo.

It was Gambrelli's role to tell the girl of Annette's murder. He began gently, taken by the uncanny resemblance between the two sisters. "*Almost like twins*," The concierge on Leopold Street had said.

Gambrelli could not help recalling the dead woman in the hospital morgue and how her beauty transcended the pallor of death. Here before him was the same image, only flush with life.

At first, her reaction to the news had been a stunned silence, followed by tears moving down her face one at a time before she succumbed to a muffled sobbing. Detective Gavros moved toward her then hesitated. After a nod of the chief inspector's head granting permission, he sat on the couch and attempted to console the trembling girl.

The men stood in silence, waiting for Lisa to look up. Gambrelli was about to speak when she asked, "When did ...?"

"Tuesday evening."

"How... How did it happen?" Lisa asked Gambrelli.

"She was attacked in her home by someone with a knife."

"Someone? Who?" She did not wait for an answer. "Has anyone told Jean Michel?"

Gambrelli could feel the eyes of his men move from the girl to him. "Jean Michel Bertrand has been arrested for Annette's murder," he said.

"Jean Michel? No. He is innocent. He had nothing to do with it," she lashed out at Gambrelli with a certainty in her voice that took him by surprise.

"The Provincial Police believe he is guilty, and they have evidence to substantiate their belief."

"They are mistaken—I know he is innocent."

"You know he is innocent, how?" Gambrelli leaned toward her.

"Because…"

She appeared to Gambrelli to suddenly change the direction of her thoughts.

"Because?" He tried to encourage her to continue along the path he feared she would abandon if given a moment to think.

She looked him in the eye. He could almost feel her mind take control of her emotions. He knew the moment of spontaneous reaction had passed. What was she suppressing?

"Because Jean Michel loved her. He could never hurt her." Lisa fell onto Detective Gavros's shoulder and began to sob.

"Did you tell anyone Annette lived on the Island of Q?" Gambrelli's voice was stern.

She pulled away from Gavros and stared at Gambrelli for several seconds.

"Why would I?"

"Did you tell anyone about the island, yes or no?"

"No, no one."

She eased forward onto Gavros's chest and turned her face from the chief inspector. The sobbing began again. Instinctively the young detective placed his arm around her and gently pulled her firmly against his heavy coat.

Gambrelli decided to wait a few minutes before advancing the questioning of Lisa Cuomo. Under other circumstances, he would have given the girl more time to compose herself after hearing the news of her sister's murder, but something told him to press on. Still, in spite of his instincts, he backed off momentarily.

He occupied himself by looking around the apartment. It appeared to him that it had once been a large room, now divided into two by a greedy landlord. The larger side was the sitting room in which they were now standing. A coffee table in front of a small couch and a table with two wooden chairs were the only furnishings. A slight indentation in the wall served as a makeshift kitchen identifiable only by the presence of two gas burners and a shelf on which sat a piece of hard-crusted bread, a ceramic container of potted meat, and a sturdy kitchen knife.

Gambrelli picked up the knife. He had seen this type of craftsmanship before. It was a country knife made from an old saw blade, shaped, fitted with a wooden handle, and then honed to razor sharpness. The weight of the blade was substantial. Not heavy enough for a leg bone, but chopping off a few fingers could be done with ease. He set the knife back on the shelf.

To his right was the room's only window. The drapes were heavy and tightly drawn. He pulled back the drape just enough to confirm that the window looked out onto the street in front of the apartment house.

He entered the smaller of the two rooms, which functioned as the bedroom. To the right of the archway connecting the two rooms was an overstuffed chair. Gambrelli had not seen it when he first entered the room as his attention was drawn to the narrow bed. He opened the closet door and found a few summer dresses, garments better suited to colder months, and a long black coat. The label of the coat showed that it had been purchased at one of the City's more exclusive department stores. The dress labels indicated that they were also from the expensive end of town. He thought briefly of the simple clothing that had hung in Annette Cuomo's closet.

He pushed the clothes to one side and inspected the tongue-and-groove floor. In the center of the closet floor was a trap door, with a small iron ring countersunk into the wood. There were no pry marks along the edge of the wooden slats similar to those he had discovered in Annette's cottage by the sea.

He pulled upward on the iron ring, lifted the trap door, and used his lighter to illuminate the space below the floor. It was a foot deep and twice as wide. Several pipes ran across the bottom of the opening. He dropped the trap in place and closed the closet door.

The sobbing had stopped, but she was still crying. He could hear Detective Gavros's soft voice asking if she was sure the descriptions of the two men who had been inquiring about her on Leopold Street meant nothing to her. Gambrelli could not hear her reply, but he knew her answer would be "no."

He inspected the rest of the room. There was no bath. He assumed there was a shared facility somewhere at the end of the poorly lit, common hallway. Next to the overstuffed chair was a small circular table on which sat a tiny lamp, the room's only light. He pulled the bedroom curtains shut before sitting in the chair and turning on the lamp. He looked toward the bed jutting out from the far wall. Above the headboard was a wooden cross, the kind that had regularly hung above the beds of children in his youth. He shut off the lamp.

While Gavros talked in reassuring tones, Gambrelli listened as he returned to wandering about the apartment. Gavros began questioning Lisa. Gambrelli let him continue as the young woman seemed comfortable responding.

Lisa said she was going to visit Annette. Her sister had returned to the island last Wednesday, but had left a black bag behind. Acting upon her sister's instructions, Lisa had put the bag in her suitcase to give to Annette upon her arrival at the Island.

Gambrelli motioned to Detective Lanier to follow him into the bedroom. "Where was she when you found her?" Gambrelli asked.

"One of the bookstore employees said he had seen her carrying a suitcase heading toward North Station. We intercepted her two blocks from there."

"Did she ask you why you were stopping her?"

"No, she never asked a thing. She just got into the car after Gavros identified himself."

"Where is her suitcase?" Gambrelli unbuttoned his coat.

"In the other room, by the front door."

"Bring it."

Gambrelli watched Lisa Cuomo as Lanier crossed the room and carried the suitcase into the bedroom. He was certain that her eyes never left Lanier once he stepped toward the bag.

A moment later, Lanier tossed the suitcase on the bed and snapped open the latch. Gambrelli turned on the small lamp next to the overstuffed chair before inspecting the contents of the suitcase. More exclusive labels presented themselves. Underneath the garments, Gambrelli found a black canvas bag.

"There are no trains to the south coast leaving from North Station," Gambrelli said quietly as if talking to himself, "To reach the island she would have had to depart from Central Station on the train to Marseilles...."

"I know." Lanier said as if the chief inspector had been talking to him. "I told her that in the car.

She said it was the only station she had ever been to and assumed it served all locations."

Gambrelli looked hard at Lanier without speaking.

"She's just a country girl, Chief. How is she to know the crazy way the government has organized the train system?"

"She looks sophisticated enough to me." Gambrelli reached into the suitcase and picked up the black canvas bag—a bag he was certain was the one Annette had carried from the Savage Gallery a week earlier.

He moved to the sitting room and dumped the contents of the black bag onto the coffee table. Five rectangular bundles, all approximately the same size, wrapped in heavy brown paper and tied with white string lay between Gambrelli and the girl. Sergeant Andres took a knife from his pocket and cut the strings on the five bundles. He removed the brown paper wrapping.

Gambrelli thumbed the edge of each bundle to assure himself they contained bank notes, each in denominations of one hundred francs or more. He estimated the total to be close to four-hundred thousand.

Lisa looked at the five unwrapped bundles of currency.

"And your sister said nothing to you about the contents of this bag?" Gambrelli asked.

"No. All she said was that I was to make sure nothing happened to it. And that I was to bring it to her when she sent for me."

"When did she bring the bag to your apartment?"

"Last Wednesday morning. She had come from the island the night before."

"What was her reason for coming to the city?"

"She said she had business here and had some people to meet."

"Did she tell you who these people were?"

"No."

"Did she stay with you on Tuesday night?"

"Yes, that's when she told me she had come to attend the business meeting…"

For a moment she was quiet as if waiting for another question. None came. Then she added another thought as if it had just occurred to her.

"And she said she had to collect back pay from when she worked for the produce import company." She picked up the empty black canvas bag and held it in her lap.

"What time did she arrive at your apartment on Tuesday night?"

"Just after eleven."

"And she stayed with you all night?"

"No, she left about midnight. She said not to worry; she would be back in the morning."

"And where did she go?"

"I have no idea. I assumed she was going to spend the night with Jean Michel." Her voice betrayed a note of panic. She began to cry again, turning the straps of the bag in her hands. "He lives somewhere in the City, but I don't know where."

"When she returned Wednesday morning carrying that bag, what did she tell you?" Gambrelli signaled to Andres and Lanier to pay closer attention to the door.

"She said we were in danger … She insisted I had to move right away, that we hadn't a moment to lose. She started putting all my things in a suitcase and in some boxes." She stared at the money on the table. "Within twenty minutes, we were in a taxi and ended up here."

"Did she describe what type of danger required such abrupt action?"

"I asked, but she said it would be safer for me if I did not know."

Gambrelli waited for her to continue.

"Annette told me to unpack. She put the bag in the closet in the bedroom under the trap door, then kissed me goodbye. She told me to keep the bag safe and bring it to her cottage on the island today."

"And the bag and the money remained under the closet floor until you put it in your suitcase today?" Gambrelli pushed back the flaps of his coat and thrust his hands in his trouser pockets.

"No, I put the bag in a box and left it with my neighbors across the hall."

"A bag with all that money entrusted to your neighbors?" He bent forward at the waist to lower his eyes to hers.

"I didn't know there was money in it." She turned toward Gavros as if imploring him to acknowledge the truthfulness of her statement.

"When did you place the black bag in the box and move it to your neighbor's apartment?" Gambrelli continued.

"Last Thursday. Annette was so adamant that I keep it safe I was afraid to leave it in the apartment, so at first, I carried it to work inside my shopping bag. But at the bookstore, I had to leave it behind the register at the front desk. I thought it would be safer at the neighbors. They're pensioners and rarely go out." She smoothed the black bag and set it on the table.

"Did you recently send a letter to Annette?"

She looked surprised at the question. "I sent her a letter on Saturday."

"And the contents of the letter …?" Gambrelli put the bundles of currency into the bag and stuffed the string and wrapping paper on top. He handed the bag to Gavros.

"Just a note to tell her everything was fine. And that I would see her soon. And I included a key to this apartment, in case she needed it."

"Did you write your new return address on the outside of the envelope?"

"Yes."

TWENTY

At Gambrelli's instruction, Lisa Cuomo put on her bathrobe and stood in front of the sitting room window. When he was sure she had been there long enough to provide an observer on the street certainty that she was in her apartment, he told her to step back and secure the curtains.

Lanier and Gavros took her across the hall to the apartment of the elderly couple with whom she had entrusted the black canvas bag. Sergeant Andres loosened the light bulbs in the lamps and overhead fixture in Lisa's sitting room.

"Chief, I think I should stay here with you. If you are right, and they come in looking for her, it would be better if there were two of us waiting."

"There isn't room for two of us to hide." Gambrelli slid his Beretta pistol into the right front pocket of his overcoat.

"I could stand in the closet," Andres said as he pulled one of the wooden chairs from the table to use as a stool to reach the bulb overhead.

"And if at the critical moment you were to shift your weight and the floorboards were to creak, then what?" Gambrelli held the chair until Andres stepped off, and then replaced it at the table. "No, Andres, this is better done by one man."

"Then let me do it." Andres stood by the door.

"Just wait across the hall and listen for my signal. I will call to you when the time is right. Do you have the girl's key?"

Andres held it up in his left hand.

"Don't let it out of your hand. I won't have time to wait for you to rummage through all your pockets." Gambrelli smiled and clapped the sergeant on the back as he sent him from the apartment.

Sergeant Andres knocked on the door across the hall. It opened immediately, and Lanier stood aside. Both men looked across at Gambrelli as if expecting him to change his mind and order them back into Lisa's apartment.

Gambrelli raised his right hand and nodded twice to assure them that he would be fine without them. He closed the door and put his hand in his pocket and felt the pistol. "What do they think; that I'm too old, too slow?" He strolled into the bedroom. "I was cracking heads when they were trying on their first pair of long trousers."

He walked around the darkened apartment. He was now convinced he had been correct: Annette Cuomo had been tortured before being killed. Until now, he had not known the reason. Since viewing her body the day before, he had speculated as to why she had been forced to endure an interrogation. But the money in the black bag supplied the reason. Four-hundred-thousand reasons.

Sometime during her ordeal, she must have told them the money was hidden beneath the floor of the closet. In their haste, her interrogators neglected to discover where the closet was located before ending her life. And so the bumbling sadists had first pried the floorboards in the cottage.

Gambrelli smiled to think of the look on their faces when the cottage floor yielded nothing. He pictured the two imbeciles looking at each other before cursing the stupidity of killing the woman before verifying her story. He imagined the frantic pace with which they must have proceeded to the shop where, again, the search was fruitless.

He corrected himself, speaking out loud, "But not entirely fruitless." It was at the shop the killers obtained the letter from Lisa marked with her new address.

Gambrelli went to the kitchen faucet. In the dim glow provided by the light of the streetlamps leaking past the edge of the drapes, he grabbed a glass at random and took a long drink of water. The taste was of metal. He spit it out then spit again. The taste lingered on his tongue and across the roof of his mouth.

He leaned on the counter in the dark staring at the front door. If he was correct, the killers would have already been to this apartment. From the return address on the envelope, they knew where it was, and they had Annette's key. What had they thought when they first spied the trap door in the closet floor? Did they congratulate each other? Exhale a sigh of relief? And what puzzled looks must have crossed their faces when lifting the trap revealed, for the second time, nothing more than rusted pipes?

"I'd given a day's pay to have seen that." Gambrelli smiled.

The remaining question in his mind was who directed them to Lisa's previous apartment where there was no closet to be inspected? Who were they working for? Surely any man capable of amassing hundreds of thousands of francs, by whatever means, would have had the presence of mind to keep Annette Cuomo alive until he knew the money was in hand. This suggested to Gambrelli that the killers were either working on their own, or at the direction of someone else, someone who gave orders but was not present at the scene of the crime, not present to prevent the premature killing of Annette Cuomo.

He hesitated to speculate. It might be reasonable to suspect that Philippe Gandone was somehow involved in the crime, but perhaps not. Gandone's search for Annette and his shady past did not place him behind the killing.

It was also reasonable to accept Major Ormond's interpretation of the evidence collected by his men. Maybe the major was correct and Gambrelli's concerns about the champagne bottle,

Annette's keys, the missing letter from Lisa, the failure of Bertrand to discard the bloody shirt and the red tie were "...of little consequence..."

"Of little consequence my ass—." Gambrelli said aloud, startling himself in the silent apartment. He knew there was more to this murder than Bertrand's injured vanity.

"But there is no proof," he whispered. "And without proof, without evidence, everything is but a mere guess, a worthless waste of time."

He needed facts, something concrete. Experience had taught him to be patient. Given enough time and effort the truth, or something close to the truth, was always discovered. He had to keep looking.

"But what are you looking for?"

"I'll know it when I see it. Where to look is now the problem."

"I've heard enough nonsense from you. Now be quite and wait."

.   .   .

One hour later, Gambrelli was sitting alone in the dark of Lisa Cuomo's tiny bedroom. He had given up talking to himself in favor of assessing his current situation. The light bulbs in the lamps and the chandelier in the sitting room had been loosened. The only working lamp was on the table next to the overstuffed chair in which he struggled to be comfortable.

At his direction the detectives had taken some of the clothes from the closet and shaped them into the form of a person sleeping beneath the covers of the bed—a child's trick that would only fool the killers for a moment. Gambrelli trusted that in the darkness of the bedroom, a moment might be enough.

Several times he had wanted to take off his heavy overcoat. It restricted his movement and had made him too warm at first. But since sitting down he had barely moved. His lack of movement and the creeping cold of the apartment eventually made him grateful for the coat's warmth.

Twice he thought he had heard a key in the lock. Twice he had felt for the pistol in his pocket. How would they do it? Would they creep in one at a time? Would the first to reach the bed discover the fraud beneath the covers before the second was fully in the room? That would be bad. Gambrelli was counting on both killers entering the room and standing on either side of the bed. That would give him the best chance of being able to surprise them before they discovered the bed was empty.

And what if we arrest them, and they never implicate Gandone? Gambrelli dismissed the thought. That was a possibility and the reason why he had insisted on being alone in the apartment. One way or the other, he would be the only one who knew if Gandone's name was mentioned by the killers in the darkened bedroom. He pulled the warmth of the coat higher along his neck.

.   .   .

He did not know if he had fallen asleep or was just lost in thought, but he had not heard the footsteps approach the apartment door. He became alert only after the key had been inserted in the lock. He heard it slowly turn, moving the tumblers into place.

The door opened without a sound. He closed his eyes and strained to listen. He heard two sets of footsteps cautiously entering the adjoining room. The air from the hallway rushed into the apartment, pushing the smell of tobacco and whiskey in advance of the intruders. The door closed. The lock clicked. Gambrelli removed the pistol from his pocket and held it firmly in his right hand.

Two men, hardly more than shadows, entered the bedroom side by side, one of them passing within inches of Gambrelli's left shoulder. Just as they passed him, they stopped.

Gambrelli held his breath. If they turned even slightly to the right, they would see him. He was at a disadvantage sitting in the chair. He should have stood behind it, his back in the corner.

They were almost on top of him. One step to the right and an outstretched arm and they would have him.

He needed to breathe. Heat was rising from his chest to his neck and face. He was afraid to exhale.

They started to move again, two steps away, now three. They were far enough in front of him for Gambrelli to regain confidence. He could control the situation, if only for a moment. Would a moment be long enough for help to arrive? It would have to be.

The men approached the bed, one on either side. The man on the right pulled something from his coat while the other reached for the blankets.

As the covers flew back, the taller man, on the right, spoke in a hiss, "Thief ... cheat me ... try to hide ... you—"

Gambrelli switched on the table lamp. The men turned, temporarily blinded by the light. The one on the left, his head a dark mass of black hair and beard, staggered back his hands at his eyes. Gambrelli looked from one to the other. A knife was clearly in the hand of the man on the right.

"Police! Don't move." Gambrelli pointed his gun at the man with the knife. He was tall and thin, the large knife held loosely in his hand, the blade a flat extension of the upturned palm. Gambrelli had seen knives held that way before. He knew the knife was in a competent, experienced hand.

For a moment, Gambrelli looked into the eyes of the man with the knife and saw a total lack of concern for the gravity of the situation. The man's expression was impassive. A thin smile on his lips, eyelids narrowing, the man appeared to be moving almost imperceptibly toward Gambrelli's position.

"You are under arrest. Drop the knife."

Neither man seemed to hear him.

As Gambrelli began to rise from the chair, the barrel of his pistol wavered. The man with the knife wasted no time. He lunged forward. Off-balance and falling back onto the chair, Gambrelli fired, uncertain if the shot hit its mark. The knife advanced. He fired again.

Gambrelli did not hear the apartment door crash against the wall. The detectives were yelling, but Gambrelli could not understand their words.

The knife came closer, and Gambrelli prepared to fire again. The man and the knife fell at Gambrelli's feet.

Andres and Lanier forced the second man onto the bed and handcuffed him. Gambrelli stepped on the fallen man's wrist and kicked the knife from his hand. The gleaming blade spun under the bed.

"Where is Gavros?" Gambrelli asked, moving his foot to the fallen man's neck.

"With the girl across the hall," Andres said. "Is that one dead?"

Gambrelli took his foot off the man's neck and bent down to check for a pulse. "No ... Not yet."

From the fallen man's coat pocket, Gambrelli retrieved a key ring that held three keys. A short chain connected the ring to a small brass seahorse, just as Joseph Krantz had described.

Gambrelli looked up. Gavros and Lisa Cuomo were standing in the bedroom archway. Gavros held the black bag. Lisa moved against Gavros, seeming to hug his waist. As Gambrelli regained his feet, a struggle began between Gavros and Lisa.

"What? Hey, stop!" Gavros yelled.

It was too late. Lisa pulled Gavros' revolver from his waistband. She pushed past the detectives and their handcuffed prisoner, moving forward, aiming the barrel of the gun at the man sprawled on the floor. Gambrelli reached for the girl's wrist, but she pulled the gun back and parried his advancing hand. Gavros swung the canvas bag. The gun roared as an orange flame burst from the end of the barrel. A split-second later, Gavros had control of the weapon and twisted it from Lisa's hand.

"He murdered my sister," she screamed, clawing Gavros' arm to recover the gun. "Kill him. Kill him."

Lanier threw his arms around the hysterical woman, pulling her off her feet and dropping her on the floor in the sitting room.

Gambrelli again checked the pulse of the man on the floor. To the left of the man's head, he saw the hole in the floor made by the bullet from Gavros' gun.

"She didn't miss by much," Gambrelli said as he touched the damaged wood. "Probably should have let her finish him."

TWENTY-ONE

Gambrelli, in his shirtsleeves and unbuttoned vest stood behind his desk. He lit a cigarette while Lieutenant Vigier, of the Narcotics Bureau, sat across from him and read aloud from a thick file spread across his lap.

"The man you shot is Jean Valier. He works for Philippe Gandone as a warehouse supervisor. The other, the one with the beard, is Raul Escobar, a ship's navigator on one of Gandone's vessels." Vigier pulled a wrinkled sheet of paper from the file. "Here is the crew list from the vessel Black Swan. It was taken by the Coastal Patrol the night she was boarded and seized with a load of opium."

Gambrelli glanced at the list then set it on the desk. He poured a finger of brandy into a glass and handed it to Vigier.

"Both Valier and Escobar are on the list," Vigier said. Referring to another page from the file, he

added, "Both were arrested and both served time...
Valier five years... and Escobar four."

"Gandone was arrested with them?"

"A few days later...He was not on the boat."

"But he was never convicted on the smuggling
charges?"

"He was never officially charged. His lawyer
produced documents proving the vessel had been
leased to a company in Argentina at the time of the
seizure...the judge ordered Gandone's immediate
release."

Gambrelli took his glass and walked to the window. He looked down at the canal where a barge
moved noiselessly in the dark. On the other side of
the canal, the bistros that catered to a late-night cli-
entele still had their lights on.

The rain had stopped. The wind was picking
up, and a low sky hung just above the top floors of
the hotels that scattered the hillside of the Central
District. The newest of the hotels, the Carlton, had
stone turrets set on each corner of the roof. From
the top of the turrets, lights pointed upward illumi-
nating the low clouds.

Gambrelli realized Vigier had stopped reading.
He wondered if the lieutenant was waiting for him
to respond to some unheard question.

"Did you ask me something?"

"I said, 'Is there something interesting out
there?'"

"I was just looking at the roof of the Carlton."

"My God, can you believe the money these construction companies must be making? It seems every day they are breaking ground for another office building or hotel." Vigier sipped his brandy. "My brother-in-law is the maintenance supervisor at the Regency, and he says—"

"The crew list." Gambrelli reached for the paper on the desk. He ran his finger across the page. "I can't believe I didn't think of this before." He grabbed the phone. "Operator, connect me to the Provincial Police on the Island of Q. Ring me back when you have them on the line."

"What is it?" Vigier asked. "What have you discovered?"

"Here on the crew list of the Black Swan, the name Beluse, Claude Beluse." He shook the paper at Vigier and dropped it on the desk.

Before Gambrelli could elaborate, Sergeant Andres entered the office.

"Chief, I've got Renard on the line; he and Bruno are with Lieutenant Vigier's detectives. They followed Gandone to a restaurant called Racine's in the North Gate District. He said Gandone has settled in with a couple of ritzy types—two bottles of champagne on the table, looks like they'll be there for a while. Renard says the place is full of dinner jackets and low-cut gowns. Do you want me to put him through to your line?"

"No, I'm waiting for a call." Gambrelli sat in his chair. "Tell Renard to contact the North Gate commander and get some uniformed officers over to the restaurant. Tell him I want Gandone arrested."

"But Valier and Escobar haven't said a word to implicate Gandone," Andres said.

"We don't need their cooperation. In fact, stop interrogating them and send them to the fortress. But first tell Renard to pick up Gandone."

Gambrelli saw a twinge of concern pass across Vigier's face.

"Sergeant, tell Renard to have the narcotics detectives arrest Gandone, and make a show of it. If Gandone gives them any reason, I want him roughed up. And suggest to Renard that it would be a good opportunity for the North Gate officers to throw their weight around."

Out of the corner of his eye, Gambrelli saw a smile form behind Vigier's brandy glass.

"And Sergeant, make sure that Renard lets that young officer that's driving him get a piece of the action."

The desk phone rang.

"Gambrelli ... Yes, Corporal, put me through to Major Ormond ... Yes, I know what time it is ... Then wake him."

Gambrelli cradled the receiver between his shoulder and his jaw as he poured another brandy into his glass.

"Ormond, Gambrelli here ... Yes, I know the time. There is a fisherman on your island, Claude Beluse. He keeps a boat at the dock near the Island Tavern. I left his name for you last night ... Good.

Have your men locate him and place him under arrest for the murder of Annette Cuomo ... Yes, I am sure he was involved ... No... not the killer, but I would guess he can testify against the men who did it. When you have him in custody tell him Valier, Escobar, and Gandone have been arrested ... Have you written those names down? No...I didn't mean that you...Yes, that's right. And tell him if he does not wish to stand with them in the executioner's chamber, he'd better tell all he knows.

"He should also admit to you that he was a maintenance man at the Parc Hotel. Search his home. You will find a passkey to all the rooms at the hotel. Also, have your men look around his house and see if they can find the bottle of Laurent-Perrier champagne, full or empty... the one that Bertrand brought to the cottage that night ... I don't remember the year, but Bertrand or the bartender at the Parc will know.

"Major, if your men find the bottle, we will need to preserve the fingerprints ... Yes, I'm sorry, I'm sure you do. Call me at my office with the results...I know you will need a warrant...There is no rush, but immediately would not be too soon... as soon as you can...Thank you Major. Wait, the champagne, it was nineteen twenty-seven."

Lieutenant Vigier rose and placed his file on Gambrelli's desk.

"I'll leave this with you." He said, pointing to the file. "I'm sure you can make better use of it than I. We can discuss it later if you like. For now, I will wait for my men and Gandone at the prisoner's entrance."

Gambrelli returned to the window to wait for Major Ormond's call. The clouds were lifting. The wind had dried the cobblestone streets on the other side of the Central Canal. He put another piece of coal in the fire and went into the detectives' office bay.

Sergeant Andres was on the phone. At the far end of the room, Lisa Cuomo was seated on a bench next to the warm iron stove. Detective Gavros stood behind her, his hand on her shoulder. Gambrelli motioned to Gavros to follow him.

From a locked cabinet, Gambrelli pulled Annette Cuomo's black canvas bag and removed several bank notes from one of the packets.

"Take this and get the girl a room. She will have to stay there for a few days until this is all settled. I don't want her returning to her apartment."

The detective took the money and folded it into his pocket.

"You will be responsible for her safety, so get a room for yourself, adjoining, if possible." Gambrelli returned the bag to the cabinet and locked the drawer. "And Gavros, you will be accountable for the money spent, so keep track."

Gambrelli waited until Gavros and the girl were gone before returning to the detectives' bay. Andres was hanging up the phone.

"Chief, I just talked to Bruno. He and Renard stopped by the hospital. Valier is stable, one round to the left arm and one hit him in the right shoulder. They say the wounds are not serious, but the doctors want to keep an eye on him for a few more hours. A patrolman has been assigned to stand watch tonight. Bruno will transport him to the prison infirmary when the doctors sign the release in the morning."

"And where are Renard and Bruno headed now?"

"They're stopping for a sandwich and a drink at the Watchman's Tavern. Renard said they really gave the patrons at Racine's quite a show during Gandone's arrest. Renard wanted you to know that the young officer you assigned to drive them will have something to tell his girlfriend when he gets home."

"And Gandone?"

"The narcotics boys are bringing him in. They'll give him the once-over and call us when they're done."

TWENTY-TWO

G ambrelli picked up his phone on the third ring.
Major Henri Ormond sounded jubilant. "Arthur,
it went as you had hoped. Beluse was asleep in his
bed when we arrived. I interrogated him myself in his
kitchen. He admitted everything and said they were
recovering stolen money for this Gandone fellow of
yours and acting on his orders.

"He said he had nothing to do with the killing; he merely pointed out Annette Cuomo's cottage
and her shop to Valier and Escobar. He does not
know what happened inside. They paid him five-
hundred francs for his effort, and promised him
three-thousand more."

"Did he have the passkeys to the hotel?"

"Yes, in a kitchen drawer. He handed them over.
Said he used them to plant the shirt in Bertrand's
room. He said it was Escobar's idea. None of them
had any knowledge of Bertrand's position as a prosecutor. Beluse had seen the victim with Bertrand on

several occasions and had seen him coming and going from the Parc Hotel multiple times over the few months.

"On the night of the murder, he followed Bertrand away from the cottage to the Parc Hotel. One of the maids gave him Bertrand's room number.

"And the champagne bottle?"

"We found it, empty, in the trash behind the house."

"Bring Bertrand to the City tomorrow on the early train. I want you to review the case. I will arrange for you to be met at the station."

Gambrelli hung up the phone and took his coat from the rack near the door.

"Sergeant Andres, care to join Renard and Bruno? I could use a bite, and I want to hear the details of Gandone's arrest."

.   .   .

One hour later, the narcotics detectives delivered Gandone to one of the interview rooms adjacent to the Major Crimes Bureau. Another hour passed before Sergeant Andres stood next to Gambrelli's desk.

"He admits to knowing Annette Cuomo, but denies everything else. Says he has no idea what we are talking about."

"And what do you think?" Gambrelli asked.

"I'm inclined to believe him. He seemed genuinely shocked when I told him Annette Cuomo had been murdered... I mean I know he's a crook, but—"

"I'll have a look at him." Gambrelli rose and put on his suit coat. He was angry with himself for not taking the lead in Gandone's initial interrogation.

"His lawyer, Malbec, is waiting in the hall. He demands to see Gandone immediately."

"How does Malbec know Gandone is here?"

"He was at the table in the restaurant when they grabbed Gandone. He knows he's somewhere in the building."

"Ignore him for now. I want a few minutes with the prisoner without interference."

The sergeant held Gambrelli in the office for another moment. "The *Times* and reporters from other papers are starting to call in. The word is getting around that Prosecutor Bertrand has been arrested. The desk sergeant called up here to see if it was true. The *Times* reporter specifically asked him if the charge was murder."

"Admit nothing." Gambrelli stepped into the hall. "In a few hours, all will be known and the vultures, reporters, lawyers, and gossips alike will have their fill of raw flesh."

At the far end of the corridor, Gambrelli saw the attorney, Malbec, sitting alone on one of the wooden benches that in several hours would be full of reporters as well as suspects, victims, and witnesses to the evening's crimes.

Malbec waved and started to rise. "Gambrelli, I want to see my client."

The chief turned his back and kept walking, ignoring the lawyer.

"Chief Inspector, wait. My client has been arrested, and I demand to see him."

Gambrelli heard the slapping of thin-soled Italian shoes closing the distance between them. He did not turn around when he heard the voice of Sergeant Andres interrupting the attorney's stride. He imagined that the sergeant's strong right arm stopped Malbec's pursuit.

Casually, he entered the corridor that was lined on one side with small rooms sealed by heavy wooden doors that deadened the sound of suspects' cries for help and their eventual confessions.

Gambrelli leaned on the table in the interrogation room. He could feel the struggle between fatigue and adrenaline for control of his brain. After twenty minutes of dancing with Philippe Gandone, he was ready to go home for the night. Like Sergeant Andres he was inclined to believe Gandone had little or no connection to Annette Cuomo's murder. He just needed to dangle the bait one more time, and he was sure the smuggler would leap at it.

Gandone, in evening dress with a white silk scarf around his neck, dabbed a monogrammed handkerchief at the corner of his bruised mouth where a persistent trickle of blood made its way along his lower lip from somewhere inside. Gandone watched the chief inspector with eyes that alternately expressed contempt and fear. To Gambrelli, he seemed a cornered animal, trying to anticipate from which direction the killing blow was to be delivered.

Gambrelli lit a cigarette and, in an absent-minded tone, addressed Gandone. "It's the money you see. All that money makes a powerful motive for murder." Gambrelli paced his remarks, forcing Gandone to wait for an opening that might allow for his escape from certain death. Gambrelli had delivered the opening, and it was his turn to wait for Gandone to take the opportunity.

"What money?" Gandone removed the scarf and examined it as if assessing the damage it had suffered at the hands of the narcotics detectives. He tossed it onto the interrogation room table with disgust.

Gambrelli saw a few blood stains and a smudge on the white silk and assumed it no longer appealed to Gandone in its state of diminished elegance.

"What money?" Gandone repeated the question.

Gambrelli ignored the question again. He wanted Gandone to have time to absorb the situation and formulate his own plan for obtaining freedom. Gambrelli changed the subject. "In what capacity do you employ Jean Valier?"

"He works for me as a warehouseman."

"And Raul Escobar?"

"A navigator, on the vessel Blue Star. It is one of my transport ships." Gandone fingered the damaged scarf. "Why do you ask?"

"We have them under arrest. They have confessed that you sent them to retrieve your money from Annette Cuomo."

"That is absurd." Gandone leaned back in his chair. "I never sent them to do anything of the kind. If they say otherwise, they are lying."

"Then why do you suppose they were at her cottage on the Island of Q?"

"How should I know what they were doing on the island? I didn't know where she was. And I did not care."

"You made several inquiries around the city trying to ascertain her location. Why."

"I wanted to see her. It is as simple as that. She was a beautiful woman."

"Nonsense. You discovered her location and sent your men to the island."

"I did no such thing."

"They were there to get your money from Annette. It is obvious. And in their effort to retrieve it, they killed her. Do not play us for fools." Gambrelli waited.

"There was no reason to get any money from Annette." Gandone took a silver cigarette case from his dinner jacket. The tension eased from his neck, his eyes softened.

Gambrelli suppressed a smile. He sat on the edge of the table and waited for Gandone to continue.

"I gave it to her. Why should I want to take back a gift?" He placed a cigarette in an ivory holder and lit it, blowing the smoke in Gambrelli's direction.

"Why would you make such an extravagant gift to this woman?"

Gandone looked at Gambrelli. A thin smile spread across his lips before he replied. "I cared very much for Annette. One might say I had fallen in love with her. I treated her badly. She left me. By the time I realized how much she meant to me, she was gone."

"And so the money was ..."

"A gift—a way of apologizing for my behavior and a symbol of my affection."

"And Valier and Escobar were not sent by you to recover the money? Perhaps you sent them after you realized the gift was, possibly, a little overly generous?"

"I know nothing of their actions." Gandone adjusted the cigarette in the holder.

"Did you tell them you had given the money to her?"

"No." Gandone tapped an ash onto the floor. "I told no one."

"Then how could they have known?"

"I met with Annette at the warehouse, in my office. It is possible that one or both of them were in the building at the time. It would be a simple matter to overhear anything that is said in the office. I really cannot say."

Gambrelli slid off the table and opened the door. "Sergeant," he called to Andres, "bring Gandone's attorney, Malbec, in here, and bring paper and pen as well." He turned to Gandone. "Four-hundred-thousand, although not quite a fortune, is a considerable sum. I guess it's a small price to pay for a life."

"Two lives, Chief Inspector: Annette's and my own." Gandone relaxed, having found a route for his escape.

"An investment in your future, I suppose?" Gambrelli made no attempt to hide his sarcasm.

"Exactly." Gandone pulled his burning cigarette from the holder, dropped it on the floor, and crushed it with the toe of his shoe.

"You will have to write a statement that specifically identifies the money as a gift, freely given by you, to Annette Cuomo," Gambrelli said.

"Gladly done, Chief Inspector," Gandone said as Sergeant Andres and Malbec entered the room.

When the statement was complete, Gandone and Malbec affixed their signatures and slid the paper across the table to Gambrelli. He read it aloud and then passed it to Sergeant Andres, who applied his own signature and the date.

"If there is nothing else, Chief Inspector, my client and I will be going," Malbec said.

"You may go, but Gandone stays." Gambrelli addressed them as he walked out the door. "Gandone will remain in custody until he appears before a magistrate in the morning."

"My client has been beaten by your detectives." Malbec grabbed Gambrelli's sleeve. "I demand his immediate release. You have nothing on which to hold him."

Gambrelli turned slowly toward the attorney, who released his grasp and started to back away as if fearful he might be struck across the face.

"Malbec, if half the rumors about you are true, I am being negligent in not locking you up as well. Fortunately for you, at this moment, I do not have the time to gather a case against you."

"That is a slanderous remark. I will sue—"

Gambrelli grabbed a fistful of the lawyer's coat and shirt and pulled him upward onto his toes. "In fifteen minutes, my men will gather three dance hall girls who have provided you with sexual favors and no small amount of cocaine in exchange for your marginally competent services. Would you like to remain in the interrogation room and wait for the women to arrive and give sworn statements?"

Malbec did not answer.

Gambrelli returned to his office, turned off the light, and headed home.

THE TIMES

September 7

JEWISH LOYALTIES

The Jewish New Year (5695) begins on Monday, September 10. Dr. J. H. Hertz, Chief Rabbi, in a New Year address to the United Hebrew Congregation:

"At no time within living memory was there more vital a need in Jewry for a rebirth of Jewish loyalties.

"The forces of barbarism are again mighty on earth. They hold undisputed sway in what, but yesterday, were strongholds of Reason and Humanity. These hosts of darkness have placed among their primary aims the defamation of the Jew and his elimination from the cultural and economic life of the peoples…"

7 SEPTEMBER

TWENTY-THREE

The next morning, after three hours of sleep and an equal number of double espressos, Gambrelli returned to Police Headquarters. As he entered the offices of the Major Crimes Bureau his secretary, Louise Gaston, looked up from her typewriter.

"Chief Superintendent Wilhelm asked to see you as soon as you arrived," she said with an apologetic tone.

"Did His Majesty say what he wanted?"

"No. The *Times* is on your desk. You might want to take a look at the front page before you meet with him."

"Why?"

Louise Gaston returned to her typing without responding. She had learned from her boss that it was a waste of time to respond to questions when the answers were obvious.

Gambrelli took off his overcoat and headed down the corridor that connected the original Police Headquarters to the new building. The addition to Headquarters had been completed in the spring of 1933. The original plan had been to demolish the old building and completely replace it with the new one. Fortunately, Gambrelli mused, public respect for tradition and the objections of influential members of the city's elected government prevented the demolition of the historic building and, as a result, the new Police Headquarters was reduced to a modern addition.

The new building had its advantages: central heating, a reliable electrical system, and an unobstructed view of the Rhône. These were things Gambrelli could appreciate. The new building also had its negative aspects, first among them was that it housed the office of the chief superintendent for investigations, Kirk Wilhelm. Gambrelli avoided the new building whenever possible.

"Please have a seat, Chief Inspector. The superintendent will be with you shortly."

Gambrelli chose to stand. He looked at Wilhelm's secretary and smiled. "Tell me, Beverly, are all subordinates still required to wait ten minutes before being ushered into the inner sanctum?"

"All of them, except you. You are the only one who has to wait fifteen minutes." She dropped her voice to a whisper. "He has been yelling on the phone all morning. I suspect you are in for a bit of a tough time." She handed him the morning paper.

Gambrelli read the headline aloud: "*Local Restaurant Demolished During Police Raid.*" He looked at Beverly, who was waving her hand up and down to instruct him to lower his voice. He continued undeterred:

> *Jules Artelle, owner of Racine's, told reporters that the Metropolitan Police stormed through the doors of his exclusive establishment late last night, arresting patrons, and causing thousands of francs in damage to his …*

He returned the paper. "Is this what he wants to see me about?"

"For starters, I'd say yes." Beverly set the paper on the floor beside her chair.

Gambrelli looked at his watch. "I'll be back in fourteen minutes."

At the end of the hall, Gambrelli entered the office of Police Commissioner David DeMartell. He breezed past the secretary, who punctuated her cheery greeting by blowing him a kiss.

"Calm yourself, Rose, I'm a little fragile this morning."

"Fragile as a block wall," Rose said.

Commissioner DeMartell was looking out his window, his back to the door, when Gambrelli entered. "Leave my secretary alone, Gambrelli," DeMartell said, turning around. "Arthur, you look terrible."

"Thanks. You look like hell yourself," Gambrelli said as he sank into a leather armchair.

"I can't sleep anymore," DeMartell said. "I doze for an hour and then I am up for an hour, then I start over again. How are you sleeping?"

"Like a log. I just don't have the time lately." Gambrelli poured a glass of water from a pitcher on the corner of DeMartell's desk.

"My wife says I'm paying for the sins of my youth," DeMartell said.

"You're paying for the sin of allowing the politicians to pressure you into appointing Wilhelm as superintendent of investigations."

"He has powerful allies; don't underestimate him." DeMartell filled a glass and sat behind his desk. "I'm not going to be around forever, and when I retire, those same politicians will anoint him as commissioner. There is little doubt about that, my friend."

"When that happens, I will retire myself."

"I would not wait too long, Arthur. When I go out the door, you should plan on being by my side, not a step behind." The commissioner set his glass on the desk. "Good work on the Bertrand case. I received an early call from Colonel Baxter, the commander of the provincial police. He was fully briefed last night by Major Ormond. He wanted to personally thank us for our assistance in the case. He spoke most glowingly of your efforts."

"That's comforting." Gambrelli refilled his glass.

"The colonel is going to send a letter of commendation for you and your men to the mayor.

That should go a long way in helping me to deflect Wilhelm's criticism of your methods. Have you read the morning paper?"

"Criticism of my methods? What does that buffoon know about investigation? I'll tell you—"

"Chief Inspector." Rose was standing in the doorway. "Sorry to interrupt, but Beverly just called. The chief superintendent is waiting for you in his office."

Gambrelli eased out of the chair and drank the remaining water in his glass.

"You're still my hero," Rose said as Gambrelli headed down the hall.

Chief Superintendent Wilhelm wasted no time with formalities. The glass water pitcher on his desk was empty, and he did not encourage Gambrelli to sit down.

"Close the door."

Gambrelli did not obey.

"I have been chief superintendent of investigations for a year. And during that time, I have patiently waited for you to conform to my way of doing things," Wilhelm began. "I am not concerned that you do not care for me, but I expect that you will follow my orders and directives. Is that reasonable?"

Gambrelli did not respond.

"Here are a number of orders and directives I have issued to each of the investigative bureaus under my command."

He shuffled the papers on his desk and finally selected one to read in a tone that reminded Gambrelli of a lecture he had received at the age of seven from a church deacon who had caught him smoking in the choir loft.

"*No investigator is authorized to travel outside of the jurisdiction of the Metropolitan Police without the express permission of the chief superintendent.*" Wilhelm held the paper up for Gambrelli to see.

"Commissioner DeMartell said he would advise you of my departure."

"It is *your* responsibility to advise me. A courtesy call from the train station would have been sufficient in this case." He selected another page. "*Any officer that discharges his weapon for any reason is to immediately report said discharge through his chain of command to the chief superintendent of his division.*" Again, he held up the paper. "Not only did you fire your weapon last night, but you wounded a suspect. And yet, I was not advised. Can you tell me why?"

"I was a little busy at the—"

"This is not the first time this has happened with you and your detectives. I have warned you before. Do you think the rules that all officers in this department are required to follow do not apply to the Major Crimes Bureau?"

Gambrelli felt no compulsion to participate in his own beating. He decided that silence was his best weapon.

"I have also issued an order that an officer and a vehicle are to remain at Headquarters twenty-four hours a day, and are to be dispatched only at my command. Yet twice in the last forty-eight hours, you reassigned that officer for your own personal use. I don't suppose there is an adequate reason for ignoring a direct order other than insubordination, is there?"

Gambrelli silently pulled at his tie and scratched the side of his neck in irritation.

"Then there is the little matter of that riot your men incited at this restaurant last night." Wilhelm tapped his finger against the newspaper on his desk. "What was this all about?"

"The men were making an arrest of—"

"I've made hundreds of arrests and never have I ever found it necessary—"

Gambrelli slammed his hand down on the desk. "Look, Wilhelm, if you've made hundreds of arrests, they must have been in your dreams." He picked up the newspaper and waved it at the tip of Wilhelm's nose. "I am not one of your clerks that you've gotten so much pleasure out of bullying over the years. And I am not interested in the fantasies about your career that you invent to entertain the wives of your political allies." He slapped the newspaper against the corner of the desk. "I know where you came from, what you have done, and how you got this job, so save your expert advice for someone else." He tossed the paper onto the center of the desk and walked out, pulling the door violently behind him.

Rose and Beverly were standing in the outer office and jumped back as the door slammed. Their combined look of shock was followed by school-girl blushing and coy smiles spreading across their faces.

"Ladies." Gambrelli nodded as he passed them. "Have a most pleasant day."

Halfway down the hall, Gambrelli passed Commissioner DeMartell.

"How did it go with Wilhelm?"

"Quite well. He commended me for the investigation and invited Marie and me to dine with his family tonight at their home."

"God, Arthur, that bad?"

"Ask him. I'm sure he's had time to catch his breath by now."

TWENTY-FOUR

When Gambrelli returned to the bureau, Major Ormond was in the detectives' bay reviewing reports. Dressed in civilian attire instead of his uniform, the major's curling mustache gave him the look of a carnival barker.

Ormond stood and heartily embraced Gambrelli. "Magnificent, magnificent work. I commend you, and your men, on a job well done."

Gambrelli pulled back, patted the major on the shoulder, and ushered him back to his chair. "When you're finished reading, if there is anything we've overlooked, please let me know and we will try to get the information for you. We can make extra copies of the photographs of Valier and Escobar for your officers to show around the Island and to Beluse for positive identification." He turned to Sergeant Andres. "Where is Bertrand?"

"In your office, Chief."

Bertrand was seated in front of the desk, a glass of water in his hand. Inspector Renard, leaning against the wall smoking, nodded to the chief inspector before leaving the room.

"Prosecutor Bertrand," Gambrelli said. "It is a pleasure to see you a free man."

"Gambrelli, I can't thank you enough." He shook the chief inspector's hand vigorously. "I really don't know what to say. Without your help I might have—"

Gambrelli raised his hand to silence the prosecutor. He filled two glasses halfway from the bottle of brandy in his desk. He handed one glass to Bertrand.

"You still have some difficult days ahead. The newspapers are already on to the case. It will be a strain for both you and Madame Bertrand. Have you spoken to her?"

"Briefly on the phone." Bertrand slumped forward, resting his forearms on his thighs as he held the glass in both hands. "I'm afraid it is over between us."

"Possibly. There is a lot to forgive on both sides, much of which will be impossible to forget, I would imagine."

"I can't stop thinking about Annette. How horrible a death." He took another drink. "Major Ormond said she stole money from a drug smuggler."

Gambrelli did not reply.

"Even though she was leaving me for another man, I can't help loving her." He looked across the desk at Gambrelli. "Does that make me a fool, or insane? Have I gone mad? I just can't feel anything but love for her."

Gambrelli let silence fill the room. He passed a cigarette to Bertrand. He then lit one for himself and poured a little more brandy into both glasses before he spoke.

"In our business, Bertrand, we like to think that we are driven entirely by the facts. We tell ourselves we never guess; we draw our conclusions from the evidence. But that is not always the case. We can't help forming opinions—one might say—as to why a person has committed the crime of which they are suspected.

"Over the years, a detective's perspective is finely honed, and he begins to have an intuitive response to people, their motives, and the probability of their guilt or innocence. It is the detective's intuition that sends him into the night to watch a particular suspect when the evidence points in other directions. It is this intuition that causes him to interview a particular waiter, or taxi driver, when there are dozens of others to choose from. I am not speaking of the gifts attributed to fortune-tellers but the combined experience of hundreds of arrests and interviews, asking questions of thousands of witnesses. Do you understand me?"

"I believe so." Bertrand drank from his glass and motioned for another cigarette. Gambrelli handed him the pack and matches.

"It is from this realm of experience, combined with what we know that I am going to tell you my speculation as to what happened to Annette."

Prosecutor Bertrand lowered his head and waited for the chief inspector to continue.

"The shop on the island was not profitable. I reviewed the accounts. Annette wanted to expand the business and bring her younger sister, Lisa, to live with her. But money was the problem, and she could not bring herself to ask you for more."

"All she had to do was ask. I would have given her the money gladly."

"You were already underwriting her business losses and supplying her with the cottage. How could she ask you to undertake the additional expense?" Gambrelli stood behind his desk and began to pace in front of the window. "No, she cared too much for you to ask such a thing. So she devised a plan to acquire the money. She decided to take it from the only source she knew would have the kind of money she needed: Philippe Gandone, her former employer and an opium smuggler.

"I assume that while in his employ, she gained knowledge of where some of his illegal cash was hidden. Two weeks ago, on Tuesdays, when she arrived on the evening train, you met her and took her to dinner. But by your own recollection, she was distracted and did not eat, and then made an excuse to leave your company and meet you the following morning."

"Yes, I remember."

"It was that night she stole the money from Gandone. She may have suspected that someone saw her or knew of the theft, but I cannot be sure. In any event, she returned to her sister Lisa's apartment and forced her to move to a new location. This was probably because Gandone knew the location of Lisa's residence and Annette feared retaliation.

"After removing some cash for herself and her sister, she hid the money under the closet floor in the new apartment. The following morning, Annette returned to the island without meeting you as planned. She could not take the chance that Gandone or one of his henchmen might see her in the City, and connect her to the theft once it had been discovered."

Gambrelli continued, never sure Bertrand comprehended all the details. He explained how Adele, first seeing Bertrand's luncheon reservation with the divorce attorney at the University Club, and then observing Annette in his arms at the train station, became convinced her marriage was at an end. He described the chance encounter between Adele and Gandone at the Savage Gallery when she imparted her suspicions as to Annette's location.

"But Adele had no way to know Annette was living on the island," Bertrand objected.

"You saw her yourself, leaving the gallery that morning and talking to a man on the corner. That man was Philippe Gandone." Gambrelli picked up his glass and carried it as he continued to pace. "We believe that Gandone sent two men to the island to retrieve his money from Annette." Gambrelli stopped pacing and watched Bertrand. "One of the men, Raul Escobar, has named Jean Valier as Annette's killer."

"They should both be charged," Bertrand said.

"That will be up to the prosecutor and the investigating magistrate assigned to the case."

"I will see to it," Bertrand said.

Gambrelli nodded then continued. "Most of what we believe is based on Escobar's statement. He said they were acting on orders from Gandone."

"Has this Jean Valier confirmed this?" Bertrand asked.

"Not yet. He's not talking." Gambrelli lit a cigarette. "They went to the Island where an associate named Beluse helped them locate Annette. Beluse admits this to be true. He also confessed that he placed the blood stained shirt in your hotel room."

"When did they get to the island?" Bertrand asked.

"Last Saturday. It was either that day or the next that Annette must have seen them, recognizing immediately the danger she was in. In a naïve effort to protect herself, she had a new bolt installed on the cottage door. Her next concern was to protect you."

"Me?" Bertrand set his glass on the desk.

"She knew you were to arrive on Tuesday. Her only thought was to keep you from whatever harm might befall her. She needed a way to drive you from the island, at the least, away from her. So she invented the story of another lover, a younger man. It was something you had suggested to her, and so it would make sense that it was a story you would believe."

"If she had only told me the truth," Bertrand said.

"She knew these were dangerous men. In her mind, to tell you would have only resulted in your being injured or killed."

Bertrand placed his head in his hands. Gambrelli stood at his side and set a hand on the prosecutor's shoulder.

"She loved you, Bertrand, possibly more than you ever suspected. Possibly more than a man has a right to be loved."

Gambrelli left the prosecutor sitting alone. As he stepped into his secretary's office, Louise handed him the phone. "It's the commissioner's secretary."

"Yes, Rose, what is it?" Gambrelli listened without speaking until he said, "Thank you, Rose, I will consider it." He handed the phone to Louise, who Gambrelli knew would not attempt to satisfy her curiosity by asking him any questions.

Gambrelli leaned into the detectives' bay and signaled to Sergeant Andres and Inspector Renard to join him in the hall.

"Do either of you remember an old prosecutor, he was a widower? He used to take the court duty for every holiday season so the others could be with their families."

"Rittman, Jacob Rittman." Renard was the first to reply.

"Where is he now?" Gambrelli asked.

"I saw him last year," Renard said. "He was having dinner with a wealthy widow at the Carlton. I think he said he had set up a practice somewhere in one of the lake counties."

"Good," Gambrelli said. "Sergeant, make a verbatim copy of Gandone's statement. Then locate Rittman and make an appointment for Lisa Cuomo to see him tomorrow."

"So you're going to accept Gandone's statement that he gave the money to Annette Cuomo?" Andres asked. "We're not going to use the theft of the cash as his motive for ordering the murder?"

"Gandone gave the statement only after it was clear we suspected his involvement in the murder, and that the retrieval of the money was the motive. His statement that the money was a gift will be laughable to a jury with Beluse and Escobar identifying him as the one who gave the order to track down Annette.

"For our purposes the statement is his admission that it was his money and he knew Annette was in possession of it. I don't think we will need the money to make the case against Gandone. In any event we can try and prevent it from being returned to him. The courts are not in the habit of returning money to criminals. Lisa might as well plan to inherit the money, or at least lay claim to it, as her sister's only surviving relative."

"But the money was stolen."

"Not according to Gandone. He can't have it both ways."

Gambrelli touched the sergeant's arm.

"Andres, I've given Prosecutor Bertrand a few facts and some nonsense to occupy his mind, and just enough compassion to make him easier to deal with in the future. Allow him a few more minutes alone and then drive him home."

"Yes, Chief," Andres said.

"I can go to the hotel and relieve Detective Gavros," Renard said.

"No. Leave him with the girl for now. But Andres, call Gavros and caution him. Although Gandone and the two killers will remain in custody, we can't be sure there aren't others on the same mission. He must remain alert." Gambrelli thought for a moment and added, "Have Detective Lanier arrange with Gavros a system of relief."

Renard looked annoyed at being left out of the mix. "I'll do it, Chief. I can relieve Gavros. I've got no one waiting at home for me." Renard's offer was almost a plea.

Gambrelli ushered Inspector Renard across the hall and into the nearest interrogation room. Once the door was closed, Gambrelli leaned toward Renard. "I've just been informed that Superintendent Wilhelm has made a habit of leaving the office at noon on Fridays. Sometimes he returns late in the day, but most of the time, he doesn't come back."

"And you want me to find out where he's spending his Fridays?"

Gambrelli smiled and nodded.

"Do you think it is a woman?" Renard asked through a widening grin.

"I think nothing at this point. I expect you to tell me what you discover."

"I'll take Detective Bruno. We can check out a car and—"

"No, do it alone. And don't use a department vehicle. Borrow a car from one of your lady friends."

"Do you want photographs?"

"If they can be done discreetly."

TWENTY-FIVE

When Gambrelli returned to his office, Major Ormond was waiting.

"Major," Gambrelli began.

"Please call me Henri," Ormond said.

"I would like you to join my wife and me for dinner at our home this evening." The words were difficult for Gambrelli, but he could not resist extending his hospitality to a visiting police officer. A courtesy, Gambrelli was acutely aware, Ormond had not extended to him.

"I would be delighted," the major replied.

"I will pick you up at your hotel at seven." Gambrelli already regretted his attempt at civility.

"There are two issues we need to discuss," Ormond said. "The first is the body of Annette Cuomo. It has been three days, and although the weather has cooled a bit, the corpse cannot remain in the hospital much longer."

"I'm sure there is a mortuary on the island to which the body can be consigned," Gambrelli said.

"Yes, there is one undertaker, but he will not take charge of the body unless he has some guidance as to what is to become of it."

"And a guarantee of payment, I assume." Gambrelli looked at the locked cabinet containing the thick packets of francs. "Contact the mortician and assure him that payment is guaranteed by the Metropolitan Police. Give him my name if necessary. I will have my detective obtain instructions for him from Annette Cuomo's family."

"I will make the call immediately." Ormond started to leave.

"Major," Gambrelli said, "what is the second issue?"

"Yes, well ..." Ormond hesitated as if searching for the proper phrase. "I noticed in one of the reports, it is stated that Claude Beluse identified Philippe Gandone as the person ordering the confrontation with Annette Cuomo."

"That is what you told me last night." Gambrelli checked his notebook: *Beluse identified Gandone as the one giving the orders.* I've noted it right here."

"Yes, well, at the time I spoke to you, that is what he had said." Ormond seemed uncomfortable. "But later, he gave a more detailed account in which he admitted that he never actually spoke to Gandone. Beluse had only *assumed* Gandone was giving the orders based on what Valier led him to believe."

Gambrelli set his lower jaw slightly to the left. It was an almost imperceptible movement that Gambrelli had adopted over the years. The detectives in the Major Crimes Bureau had learned to perceive the setting of the chief's jaw as a prelude to a tempest, a warning sign of potential doom.

"And what specifically did Valier say that led Beluse to make that assumption?" Gambrelli made a conscious effort to control his temper.

"It was nothing specific. Beluse just assumed that since Valier and Escobar arrived on his doorstep looking for Annette Cuomo, who they said had stolen money from Gandone, that the operation was ordered by Gandone," Ormond said in a matter-of-fact tone.

Gambrelli stood up and walked to the window. He looked down at the canal, waiting for the slow routine of the barge traffic to calm his temper. *This idiot*, he thought, while looking alternately between the graying sky and the café facades across the canal; *first, he arrests the wrong man, a mistake we have all made, I must admit. But then, in the face of conflicting information, he justifies his actions and defies logic. Now he has overstated the case against Gandone, a bit of buffoonery for which I must now suffer the consequences. And on top of it all, I've invited the man to my house for dinner.*

"I hope that is not going to cause you too much of a problem," Ormond said.

"No, I'll live through it," Gambrelli said aloud, immediately aware that while he was thinking of dinner, it was apparent Ormond was referring to the misunderstanding about Beluse's statement.

"I would hope so," Ormond said in an upbeat tone. "I am done with the file review. I will expect you at seven. I look forward to a good home-cooked meal and meeting Madame Gambrelli."

All Gambrelli could do was smile and nod his head as the major departed. He dialed his home. Marie Gambrelli took the news of a dinner guest with her usual enthusiasm.

"I think it's charming that you've invited him; it's so unlike you. It will be fun," she said.

"If I don't strangle him in the taxi," Gambrelli mumbled.

TWENTY-SIX

The brass lamp on his desk cast a circle of light just large enough for the sheet of paper upon which Gambrelli struggled to write a precise account of the actions of the previous evening that resulted in the shooting of Valier. Through the open door he heard the voice of Commissioner DeMartell making inquiry of Madame Gaston as to the current condition of her husband and three children.

Madame Gaston's replies sounded appreciative, but were brief; knowing the purpose of the commissioner's visit to the Major Crimes Bureau had nothing to do with her.

"I need to speak with your boss for a moment Madame Gaston. Please prevent any interruption... I'll just close his door...."

Without warning Gambrelli's memory plunged into another time when DeMartell had entered his office and closed the door. The eight year-old daughter of the Spanish vice-council had gone missing. The girl had last been seen at the garden gate of the convent school talking to a well dressed man.

The importance of the event was underscored by the fact that the missing girl's hysterical mother was a close confidant of the governor's wife, and therefore the full effort of the metropolitan police was required. The commissioner placed the entire affair under the control of Gambrelli and his detectives, pledging that all the department's resources would be available at the chief inspector's request.

Within hours the newspapers had hold of the story, keeping it on the front page of every issue. Articles appeared, filled with information, some accurate, some fanciful. Anyone who would willingly talk to a reporter was quoted at length. The veracity of their statements was never questioned by reporters or editors eager to beat their competitors with the latest tidbit.

Every article ended with a plea for the public to come forward with information. As a result the detectives were overwhelmed with burdensome tips and sightings, each one fully investigated, thereby draining all resources, and keeping the detectives without sleep for days on end.

I saw a man with a young girl... at Central Station...near the harbor...in a car headed east... west...north...it was blue...black...a yellow cabriolet...he was tall and thin...stocky...a dwarf... definitely a Spaniard...a Corsican, I think...

Throughout the city, day or night, no man in the company of a young girl could go about his business without interruption. Fathers, uncles, and grandfathers were all subject to scrutiny.

The call he had been waiting for came after two weeks of exhaustion. A farmer, living on the eastern edge of the North Gate District, had discovered a child's body in a drainage ditch. Officers had been dispatched to secure the scene. The district inspector would be awaiting Gambrelli's arrival....

"Arthur we need to talk," Commissioner DeMartell said after the door clicked shut.

Gambrelli struggled to force his mind to change course before the image of the discarded child appeared. He focused on DeMartell's movements: from the door to the sideboard, he picked up two glasses; the glasses were placed in the center of Gambrelli's desk. DeMartell sat down.

"I've just finished a meeting with Wilhelm."

"My condolences." Gambrelli poured cognac into the glasses.

"This time I'm concerned you may have pushed him too far."

"He's lucky I didn't push him out the window."

"I'm not joking."

"Neither am I." He slid one of the glasses toward the commissioner.

"He intends to file a complaint against you with the Board of Discipline."

Gambrelli took a drink. The naked foot of an eight year old girl was reflected in the dark water of the ditch. A child's pale arm —.

"Aren't you curious as to what this is about?"

"If you weren't going to tell me, you wouldn't have come here."

DeMartell picked up his drink, leaned back, and pressed the side of the glass against his right temple.

"He claims you are unmanageable... and your general disregard for department regulations is undermining the discipline, and the morale of the entire investigations division."

"Nonsense."

"I can't remember it all... There is disregarding a directive by reassigning personnel without proper authority." DeMartell waited for a response.

Gambrelli remained silent.

"There is a violation of the department regulation requiring the immediate notification of your superior after discharging your service weapon... I believe he has several documented instances of your failure to comply." DeMartell took a long drink. "He also claims multiple acts of insubordination, including one today.... Oh, and placing him in fear for his safety by your violent outburst in his office, also today."

"There is no way in hell that—."

"I should also tell you he intends to include Sergeant Duran and two of your detectives, Lanier and Bruno, somewhere amid the charges."

"What have they to do with all this."

"My guess is that if others are facing adverse action, he is confident that you will accept all responsibility."

Gambrelli leaned on the desk and stared directly into his glass, allowing himself a moment before he spoke.

"Once I explain to the board just what an incompetent—"

"If the board finds against you, Wilhelm will have all the justification he needs to order your transfer... that's his game. You'll be sent to one of the out-lying districts, as far from headquarters as possible. He will replace you with one of his followers, and one by one they will replace all your detectives."

"You would never allow that."

"Wilhelm is the head of investigations; he can do as he chooses with the personnel under his command. Once he has dismantled your bureau it will serve as a warning to all the other bureau commanders that dissent will not be tolerated."

"If he thinks he can control the dark forces in this city with his band of cloistered monks and altar boys he is more delusional than I thought."

"He sees a greater threat from crusading knights like you than from placing the populace at risk." DeMartell set his glass on the desk and started toward the door. "I'm sure you will find an opportunity to discredit him before it is too late."

TWENTY-SEVEN

The two men stood in the parlor, each holding a small glass of sweet vermouth into which Madame Gambrelli had dropped twists of lemon peel before returning to the kitchen.

"To your excellent work in concluding the Cuomo case so quickly," Major Ormond said as he raised his glass.

Gambrelli did not respond and only slightly nodded his head before taking a drink.

"I can only imagine the mess I'd have had on my hands if the case against Bertrand had proceeded. I am forever indebted." Ormond raised his glass again.

This time Gambrelli did not drink.

"There are still some issues we have not resolved," Gambrelli said.

"The murderer is in custody and his accomplice has given a statement sealing both their fates. I would say the matter is complete." Ormond refrained from raising his glass, and for a moment a flash of uncertainty replaced his smile.

"I must make a call." Gambrelli motioned toward the phone on the console. "If you will excuse me for a moment."

"Of course, my friend. I am anxious to get a preview of the night's dinner." The major walked through the dining room into the kitchen.

Gambrelli picked up the receiver. "Police Headquarters … Yes, the Major Crimes Bureau, Sergeant Andres." In the kitchen he heard his wife say "Please call me Marie," just as Andres came on the line.

"It's me," Gambrelli began. "Did Escobar say he received his orders directly from Gandone?"

"I think so. At least he said they were working for Gandone."

"Check his statement."

"Renard has it. He is in with Escobar now getting his signature on the final draft."

"Get in there and ask Escobar straight-out if he spoke directly to Gandone. I'll wait on the line." Gambrelli set down the receiver and lit a cigarette. From the kitchen, he heard polite laughter, the closing of the oven door, and the lifting of pot lids. He put the receiver to his ear and waited.

"Chief." Andres was back on the line. "He said they were working for Gandone, he's sure of it, but he never spoke to him. All his instructions were received from Valier, who told him they were to recover money stolen from Gandone. But Valier never actually said Gandone gave the orders."

Gambrelli felt his face flush and a tightening in his stomach. He looked toward the open kitchen door. "Call the prosecutor assigned to the case. Tell him to arrange for Gandone to be released immediately on his own recognizance. If he objects, have him call me at home."

. . .

They were seated at the table, a few bites into a pâté en terrine, which Gambrelli ate without tasting, nodding in agreement with Ormond's praise of Marie's culinary skill. When the phone rang, Gambrelli jumped up so quickly, the others were startled.

"Chief," Andres said, "Gandone was released this afternoon. He posted his warehouse as collateral against his bond. The prosecutor is willing to remove the bond. He said he would ask the judge to dismiss the charges completely if you insist, but that can't be done until midmorning tomorrow."

"Excellent, Sergeant. Tell him I'll have to think about the dismissal. Thank you."

Gambrelli returned to the table, his mind occupied with the repetition of questions for which he had no answer: If not Gandone, then who? How did Valier know where to find Annette Cuomo? Who told Valier that Annette was on the island? There were other questions gnawing at his brain, something he heard, maybe something he had noticed, he couldn't form them into words, but he felt them clawing their way forward.

Despite the chief inspector's preoccupation, the dinner was a success. Marie Gambrelli carried the bulk of the conversation, as was always the case. She relied upon her husband to provide a smile and a nod whenever she looked at him and said, "Isn't that interesting, dear?" Occasionally she threw Gambrelli a curve with a question that required a more thoughtful response, but he never caught the nuance and always replied with a nod and a smile.

Had the chief inspector been listening, he would have learned all anyone could possibly want to know about Henri Ormond's family, life on the island, and the major's meteoric rise through the ranks of the provincial police.

At one point, feeling guilty, Gambrelli tried to focus on the conversation. But the major's detailed descriptions of his most fascinating cases were all it took to push Gambrelli over the edge. He suppressed a yawn and made a valiant effort to appear interested. Gambrelli noticed that even the dog was forced to retreat from the table's edge and throw himself forcefully against the front door to relieve the boredom.

At ten o'clock, after a double round of goodbyes, the major was loaded into a taxi. Gambrelli returned to the kitchen where his wife was washing the dishes. He took a towel and diligently dried each one before stacking them in their assigned cupboard.

"Henri is a very nice man," she said.

"Who?"

"The *Major*." She placed a hand of the counter. "Remember him?"

"I suppose," he said, removing a black dog hair from the towel.

"It is obvious he adores his wife and children," she continued, trying to engage her husband.

"Everyone has to be good at something," he said, reaching for another plate.

"And that story of the missing brother and sister, how Henri put all his men to the task of locating them while he comforted the parents. And then after all that worry, to find the children in the gift shop trying to sell the seashells they had collected at the beach. Why, it was such a darling story."

"Touching." He put down the towel and lit a cigarette.

"Arthur, be nice." She stopped washing, "Not every policeman spends his entire career chasing kidnappers and murderers."

"Tragedy." Gambrelli poured a final glass of wine.

"You invited him, not me." She returned to the dishes. "Have you called your sister yet?"

"No, I'll do it tomorrow."

"You really should; Renelle depends on you for advice. It's the least you can do."

Gambrelli chose not to respond. He let the cigarette dangle from the corner of his mouth.

"You're lucky, you know," Marie continued. "Many people left to care for an aging parent resent those brothers and sisters who did not make the same sacrifice."

"Sacrifice?" He picked up the towel and resumed drying.

"Renelle always wanted to move to the City and open a dress shop, remember?"

"A shop that would have failed and cost her everything."

"That's not the point. It was her dream, and she gave it up to care for your father." She handed him a casserole dish. "While you followed your career, she sat night after night holding his hand when he cried in pain, changed his soiled sheets, and mopped his floors."

"I'll call her tomorrow." Gambrelli hung up the dish towel and went to bed.

THE TIMES

Police arrest murder suspects; Ile de Q murder SOLVED

Chief Superintendent of Investigations Kirk Wilhelm notified The Times that a press conference will be held at Metropolitan Police headquarters this afternoon to announce the successful completion of the investigation into the murder of Annette Cuomo.

Mademoiselle Cuomo's mutilated body was found in her cottage on the Island of Q by Provincial Police last Monday evening. Wilhelm attributes the quick resolution of the case to a joint investigative effort between the Provincial Police and a new Metropolitan Police unit operating under the Chief Superintendent's direct supervision.

8 SEPTEMBER

TWENTY-EIGHT

Gambrelli woke several times in the night; each time convinced he would remember the dream that interrupted his sleep. At five, he eased out of bed and got dressed, unable to recall his dreams.

"What are you doing up?" his wife asked.

"I'm going to work," he said.

"It's Saturday. Is something wrong?" She pulled the covers to her chin.

"I'm not sure."

After his second cup of coffee, he leashed the dog and walked across the street to the Parc de la Tête D'Or. Several days of rain had produced a morning that was clear and crisp, the kind of September day that erased the memory of August heat and prevented one from thinking of the cold months ahead. Twenty minutes later, he was sitting on a park bench with the dog sprawled across his right foot.

He thought about the previous night's dinner with Major Ormond. Actually, if he were to be perfectly honest with himself, he would have to admit he had enjoyed the evening. Ormond displayed a congeniality and humor that were totally unexpected. Gambrelli wondered how different he would be today had he signed on with the provincial police or taken a job as a country deputy instead of choosing the Metropolitan Police. Maybe he too would have entertaining stories with happy endings, stories of relieved parents and smiling children.

Instead, last night while Ormond regaled them with his tales, all Gambrelli could think of were the children he had searched for and found. His mind had flashed images of those children, of grappling hooks tearing at the flesh of their small, bloated bodies being fished from canals, of their thin arms and legs twisted in overgrown fields, where they had been discarded by a mindless predator.

He pulled his foot from under the dog, who lifted his massive head and stared at his master. "No, Odin, I don't think my stories would go well with roasted lamb and Chateau Neuf." He pulled on the dog's leash. "Let's go home, I have some work to do."

They strolled leisurely around the lake, appearing to have not a care in the world. Gambrelli, attempting to elevate his mood, made a point of wishing a heartfelt "good morning" to all who crossed their path. The dog snorted, only occasionally wagging his tail.

Near the gated entrance one of the park attendants waved and approached them at a rapid pace.

The appearance of the robust, middle-aged man brought a smile to Gambrelli's face. Most of the people who frequented the park called him 'Monsieur Robert' since 'Robert' was the name embroidered on his city uniform. Gambrelli always called him by his surname; Mordant.

Years before the arrival of Odin into the family, which caused either Gambrelli or his wife, or both, to frequent the park at least twice a day, the chief inspector had made Mordant's acquaintance after the park attendant had bravely intervened to prevent the assault of a young woman by two ruffians.

Almost every day Gambrelli and Mordant would exchange greetings, their conversation identical to the day before as if the script were written and required by some patron saint. Some time before, during or after their well rehearsed exchange Odin would release a massive evacuation of his bowels, which always caused Gambrelli some embarrassment knowing that part of Mordant's job was to scoop up and discard.

"God bless him." Mordant would always say. "If I could shit like that I'd live to be eighty." And with that said the attendant would bid adieu and pull his cart to the next stop.

This morning Gambrelli sensed something different in his acquaintance's mood.

"Chief Inspector..." Mordant called out, his trash bin, broom, and shovel rattling behind him. "Bonjour, Chief Inspector."

"Monsieur Mordant, a beautiful morning."

"I suppose you've heard all about it."

"About what?"

"Your hero here." Mordant bent forward and ruffled the hair on Odin's head and neck. "The other day when your wife was in the park... She must have told you."

Gambrelli tried to recall, but nothing came to mind.

Then he remembered Marie on the phone, '...I wanted to tell you about Odin...at the park...never mind...I'd rather tell you in person.'

"It was over there," Mordant continued, pointing toward the lake. "There is a young governess who is here often. She attends to a boy...Jules is his name, his parents...I can't think of their name... They live near..." He paused, rubbing the top of his head possibly trying to force his memory to retrieve fragments of relevant information.

The dog sat and turned his head as if he had lost interest in Monsieur Mordant's narrative. Had it not been for Marie's reference to something she wanted to tell him about the park Gambrelli's concentration would have drifted as well. In fact it may have since Mordant was still talking.

"The governess brings the boy, he's no more than four, here several days a week, and she is often met by a young man who walks with them around the lake. Sometimes they sit on a bench while the child runs about—"

"So what happened?" Gambrelli asked, hoping to move the story along.

"I was talking to Madame Gambrelli over there." He pointed, but Gambrelli did not bother to turn. "When the young woman, who had been sitting with her gentleman on the bench over there, jumps up and begins shouting 'Jules, Jules' at the top of her lungs. We all turned to look and there by the bridge, on that flat rock that overhangs the deepest part of the lake we see the child leaning over the water.

"She kept screaming, none of us moved. Then suddenly Odin broke free from Madame's grasp and ran to the rock dragging his leash behind. With a bounding leap he was on the rock and snatched the child by the back of his jacket and pulled him from the edge onto the grass. By then we were all running, but when we got there the dog was sitting next to the boy holding him down with a paw on his chest."

Monsieur Mordant was flushed with the excitement of reliving the rescue. He seemed to have more to say, but abandoned the effort. Kneeling down he took Odin's face in his hands and kissed the top of the black furry head.

"He is a hero, Chief Inspector, a hero."

Mordant rose and looked away, but not before Gambrelli noticed the gathering of tears in the man's eyes. Gambrelli also felt a wave of emotion as he looked down at the dog who was now intent on watching a squirrel circling a nearby tree.

"Well I see he has left me a present." Mordant said, pulling his cart along the path. "Back to work."

Gambrelli and Odin made their way toward the gate. They turned their heads when Monsieur Mordant bellowed out, "If I could shit like that I'd live to be eighty."

. . .

Marie was in the kitchen when they walked through the door. The dog bounded toward her voice.

"Where have you two been?" She said to Odin. "Here is your coffee, and I've some brioche fresh from the oven."

Gambrelli hoped she was talking to him.

"We've been at the park. Is there cream?"

"Oh the park..." She handed him a small pitcher. "That reminds me I have something to tell you."

They sat at the table drinking coffee and casting admiring glances at Odin as Marie told the story of the rescue of the little boy, Jules, from the seemingly horrid fate of falling into the lake.

Gambrelli was taken by the light in wife's eyes and the joy she exuded in her narration. He did his best to listen as if he had never heard such a tale of action and adventure.

Odin waited patiently between them confident warm brioche was in his future.

TWENTY-NINE

On his way out the door, he promised Marie he would be home early. He strongly suggested she take the day and wander the outdoor markets to get a healthy dose of the cleansed air.

"That sounds like a good idea. I think I will take Odin with me."

"Splendid. Enjoy the day."

He couldn't help but smile thinking that in Marie's voice there was a hint of anticipation of another heroic adventure.

Gambrelli decided to walk to Headquarters. He wanted time to think. Underneath his appreciation for the new day was a nagging concern that he had overlooked something of significance. It was a feeling he often encountered in the course of an investigation—a feeling that he never ignored. Maybe it was a word or a phrase, maybe just a glance or a guilty shifting of the eyes. He could not articulate it, but he sensed it had existed, and that he had allowed it to pass not having grasped its importance.

The questions still remained: If not Gandone, then who? How did Valier know where to find Annette Cuomo? Who could have told him? He needed time to review the events as they had occurred. He was overlooking something. He assured himself it would all be clear by the end of the day. Believing that to be true, his mind calmed and the repetition of the questions stopped.

Inspired by the weather, he took a detour through the market stalls that filled the streets along the Saône. Farmers' wives organized displays of the late harvest, while their husbands stood in small groups, smoking and lamenting falling prices and heavy rains. Older children dragged baskets of vegetables from wagons to their mothers, while younger siblings ran between sleeping horses and the wooden stalls chasing balls, hoops, and dogs.

Gambrelli made his way through the maze of country wares, ducking under the brightly colored edges of large canvas umbrellas, occasionally stopping to test the firmness of a particularly red tomato, or to check the freshness of oysters. The smell of fresh-baked bread filled the air in front of the Patisserie Lenox. He was tempted to enter the tiny bakery and grab a bag of croissants, but decided to move on in favor of an early lunch at one of the outdoor cafés along the river.

Under the shade of a yellow awning, he saw a lacquered Chinese box. He stopped and examined the intricate design painted in red on a background of black. The box reminded him that he had planned to spend the morning at the bookseller's market on the edge of the University District looking for a book he was eager to read. The previous week, he and Marie had spent Saturday night with Doctor Portiere and his wife. After an early dinner, they had all gone to the cinema to see *Charlie Chan in London*. Following the movie, they had stopped for a nightcap, and the doctor mentioned that Chan was based on a character from novels written by a man named Biggers.

Gambrelli shifted his attention from the lacquered box and searched his coat pockets for the notepaper on which Portiere had scribbled the author's name. He found the paper and unfolded it. In Portiere's illegible scrawl was written: "Earl Derr Biggers' first Chan novel: *House without a Key*."

"Is Earl a title, or a name?" Gambrelli had asked. "And what kind of name is Derr Biggers? Is it German?"

"My friend, I have no idea," Portiere had replied, admitting he had read the name in the movie review that had appeared in the previous day's newspaper.

Gambrelli decided to purchase the novel to see how his Oriental counterpart conducted himself in print. It was absurd, really, but Gambrelli had never given any thought to the idea that there were Chinese detectives. The City had a large Chinese population, yet to the best of his knowledge, there had never been a Chinese applicant to the police force.

He thought about the film as he absently turned the red-and-black box in his hands. It wasn't the crime, the mystery, or even the solution that had piqued Gambrelli's interest. Rather, he was completely taken by Detective Chan's style, his calm manner, and self-effacing smile. There were also the Chinaman's quaint sayings—proverbs, so to speak—that seemed to effortlessly sum up the situation and put the confusion of the moment into a relaxing eternal perspective. Gambrelli thought he might try that.

"You are policeman, yes?" a smooth-faced Chinese girl asked from the other side of the yellow awning.

"Yes." Gambrelli said, squinting at her, searching his memory for a glimmer of recognition.

"You are Doctor LiChou's friend; he is my uncle." The girl tossed a braid of black hair over her shoulder and gave the inspector a slight bow.

"Yes, how is your uncle?" He set the lacquered box down.

"He is in good health. He told me to look for you today and tell you to come see him soon."

"How did he know I would be ..." Gambrelli fell silent as another customer began asking the girl questions. "Tell your uncle I will see him soon."

He continued at a leisurely pace, moving along the row of stalls. The Chinese community referred to LiChou as "Doctor," but Gambrelli was never sure what type of doctor the old man was supposed to be. At one time, the chief inspector had made it a habit of visiting LiChou's herbalist shop, but he hadn't been there for several years.

"Once I've read the book, I will visit LiChou and see what he knows about Chinese detectives."

.   .   .

Police Headquarters was quiet. The desk sergeant was not at his post, and no one was in the lobby to acknowledge the chief inspector's arrival. He made his way up the main staircase, stopping on the first floor landing to light a cigarette before mounting the two additional flights.

As he entered the office, he heard voices in the detectives' bay. Sergeant Andres and Inspector Renard were discussing the case.

"What are you two doing here on a sunny Saturday morning?"

Both men appeared startled by Gambrelli's appearance in the doorway. Renard was the first to recover. "Superintendent Wilhelm just called down and requested the Annette Cuomo file. Sergeant Andres told him it was not completed, but he wants it anyway. We were just about to flip a coin to see who gets the privilege of calling you to get your instructions."

"I'll take it myself," Gambrelli said, lifting the file from the sergeant's desk. Determined not to let anything interfere with his partially uplifted mood, he tucked the file under his arm and turned to leave.

He stopped in the doorway. "So what brought the two of you into the office this morning?"

"We wanted to go over some concerns about the Cuomo case," Andres said.

"Don't go anywhere, I'll be right back."

Gambrelli set a quick pace for the superintendent's office. Without a secretary to delay his progress, Gambrelli passed through the chief superintendent's waiting room and entered the oversized office unannounced. He was surprised to find Wilhelm was not alone.

"Gambrelli, you know Captain Jergens." Wilhelm gestured toward the uniformed officer standing near the windows at the far side of the room.

Gambrelli nodded. He knew Jergens as an exemplary officer. The captain's career had been entirely within the uniformed patrol division. They had worked together in the Harbor District when Gambrelli was a sergeant, but since Gambrelli had been assigned to investigations his contact with Jergens had been minimal.

"Is that the file?" Wilhelm extended his hand.

Gambrelli dropped it on the desk just beyond the superintendent's reach. Wilhelm rose from his chair and pulled the file across the desk.

"I've been planning a change in the investigative division," Wilhelm said as he opened the file. "I am creating a special investigations unit that will assume control of cases selected from the ongoing investigations of the other bureaus. I've appointed Captain Jergens to supervise the new unit, and I will choose the investigations and oversee their development." Wilhelm looked at Gambrelli and waited for a reaction.

Gambrelli busied himself with brushing an imaginary spot of dust from his trouser leg, avoiding any immediate reaction to Wilhelm's plan. When it was clear Gambrelli had no intention of speaking, Wilhelm continued.

"There will be a press conference this afternoon at four. I will announce the existence of the new unit and will use the Annette Cuomo murder case as the first investigation undertaken by Captain Jergens and his detectives. You understand, Gambrelli, I will not mention the involvement of the Major Crimes Bureau in the matter. I want to ensure the credit for the solution to the crime will be given to the new unit, and of course, my own involvement in directing the investigation will be made clear."

Gambrelli suppressed the urge to throw a chair through the window behind Wilhelm's head. He searched his mind for a quote from the Chinese detective that would be sufficient to convey his fury. Nothing came to his mind.

He folded his hands behind his back and took a moment to compose himself before speaking. "There are several issues in this case that have not been completely resolved. To announce its completion would be premature at this point." That was the best he could do.

"I will leave the resolution of any minor problems to you. The captain and I will review the investigative file this morning. If we have any questions, I will send for you," Wilhelm said without looking directly at Gambrelli, who took the superintendent's last words as a dismissal.

. . .

By the time Gambrelli returned to his office, he had convinced himself that the politics of the department were no longer his concern. He was no longer interested in fighting every bureaucratic misstep and injustice. If Wilhelm and his followers were determined to position themselves to take over the department after Commissioner DeMartell's retirement, then what point was there in confronting them along the way?

"How did it go with Wilhelm?" Andres asked.

"He's holding a press conference at four to announce the successful conclusion to the Cuomo case." Gambrelli sat on the corner of a vacant desk and lit a cigarette.

"I saw that in the morning paper. What is all this about a new investigative unit under his direct command?" Andres asked.

"More foolishness, nothing more."

"The investigative summary in the file identifies Gandone as being responsible for the homicide," Andres said.

"Correct," Gambrelli said.

"But it needs to be rewritten. Without Escobar, or anyone else, identifying Gandone as the person giving the orders, we have nothing to tie him to the crime."

"Correct again." Gambrelli blew smoke at the ceiling.

"I told him when he called for the file that it was incomplete ... But would he listen, no."

"I told him the same thing, in almost those exact words, but as usual he is unconcerned with our opinion."

"If Wilhelm names Gandone as a murderer, there will be hell to pay."

"Correct, Sergeant. In fact, I guarantee it." Gambrelli smiled as another thought came to him. "Call the prosecutor and tell him to go ahead and dismiss the charges against Gandone. Tell him we may re-file a case later, but for now, sufficient evidence is lacking."

On the other side of the room, Inspector Renard began to gently applaud.

"Bravo, Chief," Renard said. "Well done. Now what's next?"

"Pull booking photos of Gandone, Escobar, and Valier," he said to Renard; then he turned to Andres. "When you're done with the prosecutor, call the Fraud Squad. Get a name of someone in the personnel department of Cramer Brokerage. I want to know if Lisa Cuomo has ever held a position with their firm or, for that matter, has ever filed an application for employment with them. Renard and I will take a cab to the Harbor District and get Gandone to take us on a tour of the produce warehouse. Get a car and meet us there."

Feeling a twinge of guilt, Gambrelli dialed Commissioner DeMartell's home number. The commissioner answered the phone on the first ring.

"Wilhelm is planning a press conference to announce the results of the Cuomo case. He intends to name Gandone as the murderer."

"Yes, I heard a few minutes ago," DeMartell said.

"I told him the case was not complete."

"And what did he say?"

"He ignored my warning."

"Then he will have to live with the consequences."

"It could be costly for the city if he publicly proclaims the guilt of an innocent man," Gambrelli said.

"Arthur, you must remember our illustrious Wilhelm is a very experienced investigator—if you have any doubt, just ask him. Should his actions provoke harsh consequences for the government, those who advocated for his appointment to superintendent of investigations will be held accountable for their lack of judgment."

"But you are responsible for all press conferences and—"

"Not today," DeMartell interrupted. "If you had read the department notice I sent out yesterday, you would know that I am leaving town for the weekend and have designated Wilhelm as acting

commissioner until Monday morning. All his decisions and actions are his alone to explain."

A smile spread across Gambrelli's face. "How
did you know Wilhelm is going to name Gandone
as being involved in the murder before I told you?"

"I am not as isolated, or as infirmed, as my en-
emies would like to believe. Now, Arthur, if there is
nothing else, I am taking my grandson fishing. It is
a beautiful day, don't you agree?"

THIRTY

Gandone's produce warehouse was larger and more prosperous than Gambrelli had envisioned. Groups of men were pushing hand trucks and pulling wagons overflowing with boxes of lettuce and tomatoes. On the loading docks, trucks of various sizes were being loaded with the day's deliveries. Gandone seemed to relish his role as successful entrepreneur as he escorted the two detectives and described in detail the lucrative trade in fruits and vegetables. Gambrelli grew impatient.

"Where did you stash the money?" he asked. "We have no time to watch you play the fool."

"This way." Gandone led them to the back of the warehouse, then along a narrow corridor lined on either side with wooden boxes of rotting oranges. At the end of the hall, Gandone unlocked a door that opened into a small office. He turned on a desk lamp. The back wall of the office was covered by shelves containing leather-bound account books and stacks of papers, yellow with age.

"This was the old accounting office. No one uses it anymore, since I expanded the offices on the second floor." Gandone pulled three of the books from the fourth shelf and pointed toward the back wall. "Behind those bricks," he said. "That's where the cash was hidden."

Gambrelli inspected the wall behind the shelf. Bricks were stacked but without mortar. He removed them one at a time, nine in all, revealing an opening to an iron box built into the wall. Gambrelli used his lighter to inspect the dark recess. The box was less than two feet wide and only half as deep.

"Do you check this hiding place every day?" Gambrelli asked.

"No, rarely."

"So it was mere coincidence that you discovered the theft the morning after it occurred?"

"There was no theft. I told you, I gave the money to Annette as a gift."

Gambrelli's voice was a growl. "Gandone, I am perfectly willing to accept, for now, your ridiculous story. But I warn you, if you do not tell me what I want to know, I will see that this matter dangles you near the executioner's door."

Gandone appeared to consider the chief inspector's words. Then, with a shrug of submission, he said, "When I got here last Wednesday morning, about six, the night watchman was nowhere to be found. My first thought was that he was checking the outside loading docks, but when I did not see him by six thirty, I came in here and found the money was gone."

"And the night watchman?" Gambrelli asked.

"I don't know. I sent Valier to his home to see if he was there. His wife said she was expecting him for breakfast. He had left the previous day, at his regular time, but did not return."

"And have you spoken to him since then?"

"No. He has never come back to work. I went to his home last Friday and spoke to his wife. She had still not seen him. I told her to report his disappearance to the police."

"And did his vanishing at the same time the money was taken make you suspect him?"

"At first, then I remembered. Chief Inspector, I told you I gave the money to Annette," Gandone said with a smile.

"And I told you to drop that game and come clean."

"Sorry," Gandone said, "I'd forgotten our new arrangement."

Gambrelli ignored the comment and continued to make notes. "Why did you go to the Savage Gallery that Wednesday morning?"

"Annette was the only one who knew about this box. Once, while she was working here, I was pulling out some cash, and she came up behind me. She acted like she didn't see, but I was always sure she had." Gandone pulled the left cuff of his shirt-sleeve from under the edge of his suit coat. "I went to the gallery to confront her ... she wasn't there ... I left my number with the gallery owner."

Gambrelli waited.

"Later that morning, I went to Annette's apartment. The concierge's wife told me she had moved away."

"Did she say where Annette had moved?"

"She said she did not know. I left her with a hundred franc note with my number written on it and told her there would be more money if she called with information."

"Did you make any other inquiries about Annette, or discuss her with anyone?" Gambrelli asked.

Gandone seemed to be searching his memory. "Yes, after I left the gallery, a woman came up to me on the corner and said she was looking for Annette too."

"Did she suggest where you might find her?"

"No, but she said her husband was in government service and might be able to locate her."

"Did you give this woman a hundred also?"

"No, she was obviously a woman of means, but I did give her my card."

They made their way to the front of the warehouse where Sergeant Andres was waiting. As they stepped into the bright morning light, Andres pointed to Inspector Renard's left pant leg. They all turned their heads to look at the leg, which had several stripes of white powder forming hash marks on the otherwise impeccable black cloth.

"What the ..." Renard slapped at the white marks, causing the powder to swirl in the sunlight.

"Don't worry," Gandone said, "it's only the powdered mold from the crates of rotting oranges we passed in the hall." He bent to help swat at the dust, but Gambrelli pulled him back by the shoulder.

"What is the watchman's name and address?" Gambrelli asked.

"Lonny Ferris. He lives in one of the row houses on rue Carrosse, just on the other side of the rail yard, number seventeen." He extended his arm to shake the chief inspector's hand.

Gambrelli ignored the gesture. Before turning toward the car, he said, "Tell your lawyer, Malbec, that he can earn his money by attending a press conference at Police Headquarters at four this afternoon."

Gambrelli climbed into the back of the police car while Renard in the front seat continued to slap at his trouser leg. Andres started the engine and drove off, leaving Gandone waving as if bidding farewell to relatives departing after a holiday meal.

A few blocks later, Andres turned to the chief inspector. "I met with the personnel officer at Cramer Brokerage. We went through his applicant files. There was no paperwork on file for Lisa Cuomo. He said he never heard of her."

"That's too bad," Gambrelli said quietly as he watched the passing traffic.

"As I was leaving the office, there was a call from the concierge at Lisa's former apartment. His wife wants to talk to you," Andres said.

"About what?"

"He wouldn't say, just that she would be in all day waiting for you."

Gambrelli lit a cigarette, exhaling the smoke through his nose. He tapped the fingers of his left hand against his knee in time with a melody that occupied his brain. He thought it might be Mozart.

.   .   .

They reached the part of rue Carrosse that seemed the most likely to contain house number seventeen. If the Ferris house was there, it was hidden among dozens of identical structures that stood shoulder to shoulder, stacked along both sides of the street for several blocks. All the buildings were in need of repair, and the soot from the locomotives in the rail yard clung to the facades like a black-and-gray veil.

Andres drove slowly along the avenue, waiting for unsupervised children to get out of the way and searching for number seventeen. He parked the car near a corner where the number twenty-five was scratched into the wooden door. They walked along the sidewalk counting backward until they stood before the door they all agreed must be number seventeen. Gambrelli climbed the swaying iron stairs and knocked.

A woman, not more than thirty, opened the door. She held a crying child against her left hip while another pulled at the hem of her skirt. Her light brown hair was twisted up and pinned to the top of her head. Errant strands fell from several places and, in a seemingly random and unintended fashion, framed her delicate face. Her eyes had no sparkle; the darkened flesh of worry and despair encircled them.

"Police," Gambrelli said, displaying his identity card. "We're here to talk to you about your husband."

"Where is he? Did you find him?" She leaned to her left, handing the baby to an older child who had been hiding behind the door.

"No, Madame, we have not. May we come in for a moment?"

She turned and walked into the house without answering, leaving the door open for them to enter. Gambrelli followed, passing at least one other child hiding behind a chair near the staircase to his right. The furniture and rugs were worn but cleaner than Gambrelli would have guessed judging from the exterior of the building.

They were seated around the kitchen table. She offered them tea. They declined, but she insisted. Gambrelli saw it more as a matter of pride than hospitality.

The children, however many there were, quietly amused themselves in the other room. She set a plate of tea biscuits on the table. Andres reached for one but withdrew his hand after a glance from Renard.

"When was the last time you saw your husband?" Gambrelli asked, taking a notebook from his pocket.

"A week ago last Tuesday." She glanced at a photograph on a shelf above the counter. It was a faded picture of a very young man wearing a navy seaman's uniform.

"Is that Lonnie?"

"Before he left for the war." She smiled slightly.

"What time did he leave the house last Tuesday?"

"At five, his usual time."

"How long has he worked for Gandone?"

"Five years."

"And before that?"

"He was a blacksmith's apprentice. But with fewer horses, over time there was less work. Finally the smith had to let him go." She sipped her tea. "We planned one day to return home where horses are still plentiful, and Lonnie could set up his own shop." She dropped her head slowly.

"Has your husband ever gone off before, maybe for a few days without—"

"No, and he's not a drunkard or a runner with other women, if you're going to ask. I already told the same to the police."

"What police?" Gambrelli pushed his cup away.

"At the station, last Friday, when I made a report." She straightened in her chair and pushed a strand of hair behind her ear. "Lonnie is not like that; he's a proper family man. I know how policemen think, but you're wrong. All of you are wrong about my Lonnie."

"Are you sure it was last Friday?"

"Right after Mr. Gandone was here. He's the one who insisted I make the report right away."

"Was he alone when he came?"

"Yes … and quite a fine man he is … very concerned about Lonnie and us … Gave me some money to hold us over till Lonnie got back. He had said it was wages he owed Lonnie. I took it. I know it was more than Lonnie had earned and told Mr. Gandone just that. He said I was mistaken and told me to call him if we needed anything."

"Does your husband own a car?" Gambrelli took up the notebook again.

"No, he walks to work. It's not far if you cut through the train yards."

"Papa went with a man in a truck," said a small voice from behind the detectives.

A girl, not more than six or seven, in a dress that matched the pattern and cut of her mother's stood in the doorway between the kitchen and the parlor.

Gambrelli turned in his chair and extended his arm toward the girl. "Come here, child," he said softly. "Did you see the man with the truck?"

The girl nodded but did not come closer. Gambrelli looked at her mother, who shook her head as if to disavow any previous knowledge of the girl's information.

"What did the man look like, child?" He dropped his arm to his side, acquiescing to the girl's desire to remain at a distance.

"He was much bigger than Papa, and he had no hair. I saw him take off his cap and rub his head when he got in the truck."

Sergeant Andres removed the photographs from his pocket and knelt in front of the girl.

"Look at the pictures," Gambrelli instructed. "Tell us if you see the man with the truck."

She pointed to the photograph of Valier.

Andres handed it to Gambrelli, who in turn showed it to Madame Ferris. She shook her head no.

Gambrelli turned the photograph to the little girl. "This is the man that drove away with your Papa the night he did not come home from work?" He held the photo closer to her.

"Papa comes home in the morning," the girl corrected, "but after he went with that man"—she pointed again at the photograph of Valier—"he did not come back."

Gambrelli handed the photo of Valier to Andres, who still knelt beside the little girl.

"Madame Ferris, I will need a recent photograph of your husband."

"I gave the only photograph I have to the police on Friday when I made the report." She looked at the picture on the shelf, and her eyes began to well with tears.

"We will look into this matter," Gambrelli said, more to distract than to reassure. "And I will see to it you are notified of anything we learn." He stood and led his men to the door. "Thank you for the tea."

THIRTY-ONE

Gambrelli checked his watch. Twenty minutes. He had been waiting twenty minutes for Renard and Andres to retrieve the report and photograph Madame Ferris submitted to the Harbor District desk sergeant the previous Friday. He got out of the car and entered the district building. The desk sergeant was going through a stack of handwritten reports. Renard and Andres were searching in a box containing reports as well. The three men stiffened when they saw Gambrelli approaching.

Determined to control his temper and mask his annoyance at the delay, Gambrelli attempted to don the persona of the Chinese detective, Chan. "Gentlemen, can I be of some assistance in locating the report?"

Andres and Renard exchanged questioning glances. The desk sergeant was the only one to respond.

"Good morning, Chief Inspector. We've found the report the woman made." He tapped the document on his desk. "Now we are looking for the log sheet to determine if Ferris's description has been forwarded to the other districts and the morgue."

"And my inspectors have agreed to help you locate your misplaced administrative paperwork. How very thoughtful of them," Gambrelli said calmly.

"Actually Chief," Andres said, "we're looking for a follow-up report by one of the officers who did some checking on Ferris last Saturday."

"Isn't it procedure to attach those reports to the original complaint?" Gambrelli smiled at the sergeant.

"Generally," the sergeant said, "but this is the Harbor District; things can get pretty hectic here."

"Yes, I suppose they can," Gambrelli said. "And why wasn't the report handed over to a detective for the follow-up?"

"In this district, detectives can't be expected to chase after every man who decides to take a few days off from a house full of mouths to feed."

"Yes, I suppose that's true." Gambrelli nodded and walked slowly away.

Stepping outside into the sunlight, Gambrelli felt slightly uplifted. He was completely relaxed, not in the least tense or annoyed. He had to admit to himself that there was a lot to be said for approaching life the Chan way.

Fifteen minutes and two cigarettes later, Gambrelli threw open the district's heavy wooden door and approached the three men again. The sergeant smiled. Andres and Renard braced themselves.

"Hell, man, I could have driven the report to every district in the city in the time I've wasted here. A sergeant and two detectives spending the morning looking for a damn piece of paper we don't need." He set his jaw and looked at his two men. "Get in the car."

He returned outside with the same force that propelled his entry. Settling into the back of the car, although not as calm as before, he was still at peace. He felt more himself. As the police car pulled onto the street, he wondered if Chinese detectives ever ran out of patience.

"Chief, are you feeling all right?" Sergeant Andres asked from behind the wheel.

"Drop me at Lisa Cuomo's former apartment house on Leopold Street."

"I was just wondering if you were maybe catching a bit of a cold. Back there at the district you seemed a bit … I don't know exactly, but—"

"I want the two of you to canvas the districts. Make sure they are familiar with Ferris. Then check the morgue. If they haven't been alerted, go through their intakes of unidentified and unclaimed bodies." Gambrelli avoided looking at the men in the front seat.

"You don't want us to wait for you on Leopold?" Renard asked without turning around.

Gambrelli felt no need to answer. He had given his instructions; there was no room for discussion. He realized the way of the Chinese detective could never be his way.

THIRTY-TWO

The concierge's wife dismissed her husband with a glance. Grabbing Gambrelli by the arm, she ushered him to the couch near the window of the front room. He was surprised at the force with which she pushed him down.

"I cannot tell you how excited I am to meet you, Chief Inspector." She followed him onto the couch, sitting close enough to his right side to trap the edge of his coat beneath her considerable thigh. "I read all the articles the papers write about your cases... faithfully... never miss a one."

"Your husband said you had some information regarding a former tenant, Lisa Cuomo." He inched a bit to his left to place some distance between them.

"My husband is correct, for a change." She recovered the distance by turning toward him. "The others on the street, the other concierges, will be so envious that you are here. Every time something happens in the area, they all say, 'If they would only put Chief Inspector Gambrelli on the case, we could rest at night,' and I'll tell you, I'm not ashamed to admit I feel exactly the same way."

"This district has some very fine officers." He unbuttoned his coat and shifted in his seat.

"Then why is it they never catch anyone? Burglaries, purse snatchings, a woman was attacked just last week coming out of the market. They almost tore the poor dear's arm off pulling at her purse and hitting her all the while. And who have the police arrested? No one, that's who. No one.

"Ernesto, the concierge at the Bel Aire across the street, says that you will be retiring soon. That's not true, is it?"

"Everything must come to an end someday."

"But not soon, Chief Inspector, not too soon."

"I promise, not before I hear what you have to tell me."

"Yes, well"—she adopted a business-like attitude—"the girl, Lisa ... I was coming home from the market, the same one on Beacon Avenue where the woman's purse was stolen. As I walked up the street, I saw her talking to a man." She looked at Gambrelli as if she had just given him the key to a long-unsolved riddle.

"And it was unusual for her to talk to a man?" My patience must also come to an end, he thought.

"Maybe not, but this man... he was big—very big—and ugly. Even from down the block, he looked grotesque." She jumped up and headed toward the kitchen. "His picture is in the late morning edition.

I couldn't believe it when I saw it. That is why I told my husband I must speak with you immediately."

Gambrelli pushed off the couch and followed her, eager only to avoid being trapped again by her annoying proximity.

"Here," she said, thrusting the newspaper into his hand. "The one on the left."

"This one?" Gambrelli pointed to the photograph of the prisoner Valier. "Are you certain this was the man?"

"Who could mistake a face like that?" she said, pushing her own finger at the photo.

Gambrelli sat at the kitchen table and took his notebook from his pocket.

"What day was this?" His voice lost all hint of pleasantness.

"A week ago yesterday, last Friday."

"At what time?"

"At one o'clock." She became more timid. "Yes, at one. I always go to the markets Friday at eleven thirty, and I'm home by one."

"Did Lisa arrive with him?"

"No. I saw her walking ahead of me. I was trying to catch up with her to ask why she moved out so unexpectedly. She had left in the middle of the night just two days before." She shook her head as if bewildered. "This man"—she pointed again at the paper—"was behind a tree, the one to the left of the front walk, and stepped out and took her by the arm. At first I thought it was another hooligan grabbing a purse. I was about to yell for help when he let her go and they started talking."

"Did they see you?"

"No. And to be sure, I crossed the street and watched from the vestibule of the Bel Aire."

"How long did they stand there?"

"Not long. Lisa was pointing up at her apartment. Then she went into the building. I waited a few minutes, then crossed the street and walked past the man. I only glanced at him. He didn't look at me."

"Did you see Lisa come back out and meet with him?"

"Oh, no, she was gone. I went to her apartment; no one was there. A few minutes later, the man came in asking for her. I told him she was gone. He asked where with a look and voice that could frighten the pope. I told him she must have gone out the back. And off he went, down the hall, across the yard, and into the alley."

"Did he come back?"

"Not until yesterday, at least according to my husband." She pointed again at the paper this time pointing at the picture of Valier and then the photo of Escobar. "The two of them were here pretending to want to rent the girl's apartment. Queer business, if you ask me."

"Do you wear glasses?"

"What?"

"Do you need glasses to see clearly?"

"For reading, yes. Why?"

"No trouble with seeing at a distance?"

"Oh, right. No, clear as a bell. My doctor says my eyes are as good as a person half my age." She pushed strands of gray hair from her face. "He can be called to testify to that."

"I doubt if that will be necessary."

"All the same ..."

"Were there any other men who came 'round to see the girls?" Gambrelli set the newspaper on the kitchen table.

"A while back, when Annette lived here— God, it is simply awful to think she has been ..." She ran her left hand across the front page. "When she lived here, there was a man—older, maybe fifty or so— who would come by in the evening."

She exhaled heavily and then described Jean Michel Bertrand as accurately as Gambrelli could have done. There was nothing wrong with this woman's eyesight, or her memory, Gambrelli thought.

"But after Annette moved out, I don't think I saw him again. He was quite a gentleman. He never went up to her apartment that I know of. He always waited out there in the lobby for her to come down. Sometimes I would visit with him. We would talk about the news. Once we talked about you." She paused as if waiting to be sure she had the chief inspector's attention. "It was the day the papers had the story of the murdered countess, the one who had her art collection stolen. Her nephew was accused, about to stand trial." She looked at Gambrelli.

"I remember," he said, returning his notebook to his pocket.

"So the very day they were to put the boy on trial, you arrested the real killers and recovered all the paintings."

"Not all of them." He stood and buttoned his coat.

"'The right man for the job' was what Annette's gentleman had said."

"Really, how nice of him."

"He said a man was lucky in life if he ever found the one job he was meant for. 'We are all fortunate Inspector Gambrelli found the job for which he is perfectly suited.' That's what he had said." She walked Gambrelli to the door. "Kind of a stodgy way to put it, but I agree."

Gambrelli was midway through the foyer when the concierge's wife pulled his sleeve.

"There was another man, the day after Lisa moved out, who came looking for Annette," she said, a little out of breath. "He gave me a hundred franc note with his phone number written on it and told me to call if I heard from Annette."

"Did he ask about Lisa?"

"No, he never mentioned her." She held out a slip of paper. "This is the number he wrote on the note."

Gambrelli recognized the number as belonging to Gandone's warehouse. He had no doubt she would describe Gandone perfectly.

"When will I have to come to court?" she asked.

"We will see," he said, pushing past her into the lobby.

"I'll walk you out." She took his arm.

"That won't be necessary."

She held firm. "Shouldn't I give a sworn statement?"

"I may send a man around later." He pulled his arm free, but she stayed at his side as he stepped outside.

She waved to a man across the street as she reached for the chief inspector's arm again. "There is the concierge from the Bel Aire. I will introduce you."

"Madame." Gambrelli squared himself in front of her to stop her progress. "This is a murder investigation. We must be discreet."

"Yes, I agree"—she leaned around Gambrelli and waved again—"but it will only take a minute."

"One more thing." Gambrelli stepped back. "You said the man looking for Annette gave you a one-hundred franc note with his phone number on it. Do you still have the note?"

"It may have been spent at the market." She stopped waving.

"Yes, I'm sure that it may have been." He headed down the street, leaving the woman behind.

THIRTY-THREE

Jean Michel Bertrand opened the door. "Chief Inspector, how good to see you." He energetically shook Gambrelli's hand. "Come in, please, come in."

"Your wife?" Gambrelli said as he followed Bertrand into the study.

"Gone to the market."

"The servants?"

"We gave them the weekend off. Hard to talk with the padding of feet in the next room." Bertrand sat and indicated a chair for Gambrelli. "I am truly glad to see you. I was just this moment thinking that you are the only person I can talk to right now. I mean *really* talk to."

"This is an official visit," Gambrelli said before Bertrand could become too familiar. "I'll be brief."

"Please take your time. I've no one I care to visit with, and yet being alone is stressful." Bertrand took a cigarette from a desk drawer and offered one to Gambrelli.

"Thank you, no." Gambrelli waved him off and took a cigarette from the pack in his pocket. "I was wondering, didn't you tell me that you had been to Annette's apartment on Leopold?"

"Yes, several times." Bertrand struck a match and lit Gambrelli's cigarette before lighting his own.

"I mean inside her apartment, not waiting in the lobby of the building."

"Yes, I'd been inside." Bertrand threw the match in the fireplace. "Actually, I would have never gone up to the apartment, but Lisa would insist. She would come down to the lobby and practically drag me to the elevator. She said it was silly to wait on the cold lobby bench when I could be comfortable upstairs."

"And you would wait in the apartment with Lisa until Annette arrived?"

"Yes."

"Did Annette approve of arriving home to find you alone in the apartment with her sister?" Gambrelli looked for an ashtray.

"At first she seemed not to mind, but the third or fourth time, she was a touch annoyed." Bertrand produced an ashtray from the same desk drawer and placed it between them. "I then made it a habit not to arrive until I was certain Annette was home from work and ready to go out."

"Because you, too, were uncomfortable being alone with Lisa?"

"Because it seemed to upset Annette."

Gambrelli looked directly at Bertrand without blinking, waiting for him to continue.

"Well, yes, to be honest, I was a little uncomfortable. Lisa was a little too forward."

"In what way?"

"I hardly knew her, you know, and yet she would reach out and touch my hand, or sit next to me and touch my cheek when I was talking. I found the whole thing a little disconcerting. Inappropriate, I'd say."

"Did you tell Annette about your discomfort?"

"No, I never did. I felt it wiser not to. It may have all been my imagination and the girl meant nothing by it."

"After Annette moved to the Island of Q, when Lisa would show up unexpectedly at lunchtime and you had meals together and walks in the park, did you tell Annette about that?"

Bertrand did not answer. He stared at the fireplace.

Gambrelli waited.

"Would you like a glass of wine, Chief Inspector?"

"Did you take Lisa Cuomo as your lover?"

"No, never," he said, turning abruptly from the fire. "But you are correct, I never told Annette anything. How could I tell her I believed her sister was trying to seduce me?"

Gambrelli crossed the room to the fire. He disliked this time in an investigation. Gathering the last shards of pottery, he called it. He much preferred the first few hours of an investigation.

When he was first called to the scene of a crime, when he walked into a room, a body on the floor, the clues still to be gathered—that was when he felt the wonder of his profession. Facing the empty canvas in a world of limitless possibilities filled him with anticipation. Could the crime be solved? How would he proceed? Along what streets would he travel? Who would fall under suspicion: a desperate husband, a greedy son, a jealous suitor, possibly a foreign-born prince, or maybe a seemingly harmless neighbor living just across the street who, for months, watched through lace curtains as his victim went about her simple life? Into what hidden caverns in the mind of a killer would he be forced to peer?

Patiently Gambrelli would wait as evidence was collected and statements were taken. Patiently he would watch as information began to narrow the width and breadth of his world. As the suspects were identified, his interest in particulars would increase. His excitement would race as the trail led ever closer to the guilty.

Then all at once, he would understand, often before the evidence provided the answer. In his mind, he would know the identity and motives of the killer. From that moment on, his interest in the case would wane. From that moment on, it was simply a matter of gathering the shards.

"May I use your telephone?" Gambrelli turned from the fire and dialed. He lit another cigarette as Sergeant Andres was called to the phone at Police Headquarters.

"Chief, we've got a body here in the morgue that could be Ferris. The head's been bludgeoned and the throat slit, but Renard and I think it's him."

"When was the body brought in?"

"Sunday. A young couple looking for a secluded picnic spot came across it a few yards off Brittany Road."

"Bring Madame Ferris in to identify the body." Gambrelli glanced at the fire. "And take along a matron to stay with the children until their mother returns home."

He dialed the operator and asked to be connected to the Carlton Hotel. The hotel switchboard transferred the call to the room registered to Detective Gavros.

Detective Bruno answered the phone. "I was just getting a little sleep, Chief. I had the watch until dawn."

"Where is the girl?"

"Gavros took her down to the lobby for lunch."

"Go down and join them. Don't let the girl out of your sight. When they've finished their meal, I want all three of you to return to Headquarters."

"Is there something wrong, Chief?"

"Something is always wrong. Don't be later than two."

Bidding Bertrand goodbye and promising to call again, Gambrelli set out on foot, intent on absorbing the midday sun. Somewhere in the course of the last several hours, he had lost his good mood. He found himself disconnected from the joy of the day he had felt so strongly that morning. He wanted to recapture the feeling, but his attention was elsewhere. He passed trees and shrubs, some with leaves still vibrant green, some already turning pale. They brushed the sleeve of his coat unnoticed. Had he given them a moment's thought, he would have seen them as harbingers of the gray, cold, sunless months to come.

Ten minutes later, he gave up trying to raise his mood by walking and hailed a taxi.

THIRTY-FOUR

Immediately upon returning to his office, Gambrelli closed his window. He felt chilled. From a desk drawer, he took a bottle of brandy and poured three fingers' worth into a water tumbler. His neck and back ached. He put a hand against his forehead. It felt hot. Maybe his hand was cold. He drank half the glass in one swallow.

For the next hour, he sat at Louise Gaston's typewriter and set out the salient facts in the Annette Cuomo murder investigation. Just before two o'clock, Andres and Renard walked into the detectives' office bay.

"Oh, it's you Chief," Andres said. "I heard the typing—"

"Did she identify the body?"

"Yes, she was positive. We just dropped her off at home and—"

"Write it up: the interview with Madame Ferris, the identification of her husband's body, all of it. And include the report she filed with the Harbor District. And don't forget the child's identification of Valier as the man who drove off with her father the night he disappeared. I will need it as soon as you are finished."

Inspector Renard came to the doorway brushing at his pant leg and jacket.

"When you are done beating at your clothing, help Andres with the reports," Gambrelli said.

"It's that damn mold, it won't come off," Renard said as he returned to his desk.

Andres stood in the doorway without moving. "Chief, are you all right?"

"Stop inquiring as to the condition of my health and get that report done."

As Gambrelli read the last few lines he had typed, trying to regain his train of thought, he could hear Renard slapping at his trouser leg in the next room. He reached for the phone.

"Desk Sergeant, please." He leaned back until he thought he heard one of the wooden legs of Madame Gaston's chair creak. He thudded forward as the desk sergeant came on the line.

"Duran...Is Wilhelm's driver there? I have an errand for him to run. Put him on the line."

Gambrelli waited, he couldn't remember the officer's name. When the young man picked up the phone he identified himself, but Gambrelli forgot the name as soon as it was spoken.

"This is Gambrelli...Go to Gandone's warehouse...Tell him to give you three of the rotten

oranges from one of the crates in the rear hallway...
Yes rotten...Bring them to my office...and be quick
about it."

Gambrelli returned to his typing.

Twenty minutes later the young patrol officer
arrived carrying a crate of oranges with a small bag
on top.

"The rotten ones are in the bag," the patrolman
said, placing the crate on the edge of the desk.

Gambrelli took the small bag and examined its
contents.

"What's this?" He pointed to the full crate of
fresh oranges.

"Monsieur Gandone sent it for you and your
men."

"Return it to him."

"But he was most insistent. He said they are the
sweetest, from Valencia, and—"

The chief inspector's glance was so severe that
the patrolman almost dropped the crate in his rush
to remove it from Gambrelli's sight.

·   ·   ·

At two fifteen, Detective Bruno walked in.

"Didn't I say to be here by two?" Gambrelli
pulled the sheet from the typewriter and walked
back into his office. "Where is the girl now?"

"Gavros has her in interview room one."

"Bring her here." Gambrelli sat at his desk and
finished the second half of the brandy.

Lisa Cuomo was holding Detective Gavros' left arm as they entered the chief inspector's office. They were both smiling. Gambrelli was not. He lowered his brow as he scrutinized the couple approaching him. Under different circumstances, they might well have been headed into a bistro for an afternoon glass of Pernod, or some hot cocoa.

"Sit, Mademoiselle Cuomo." He indicated the chair to his left. "Detective Gavros, get Bruno in here."

Lisa Cuomo took the assigned seat. They sat in silence until Bruno and Gavros entered. The two detectives stood against the wall to Gambrelli's right.

"Chief Inspector," Lisa began, "I would like to thank you for all your courtesies. Detectives Gavros and Bruno have been most—"

Gambrelli raised his hand to silence her.

"Thank you, I will make a notation in their files." The tone of his voice and his gesture were deliberately rude. He was tired of the game and wanted to end it swiftly and surely. Neither detective moved.

Gambrelli opened his desk to take a cigarette, but decided against it. He wanted no distractions. He began again, this time his tone was that of an elderly uncle talking to a favored niece.

"It must have been difficult for you during your mother's illness as her only caretaker, being called to do her bidding night and day, putting your dreams on hold—dreams of moving to the City, starting a career."

"I didn't mind. I—"

"Please, Mademoiselle, I am not unfamiliar with the spirit of young women. I know how isolated you must have felt, confined to a small house in a tiny village, watching your classmates go off in search of their futures while you were forced to remain behind. Even your sister abandoned you."

"She came when she could. She sent money ..."

"She came when it was convenient." Gambrelli shifted his tone to that of an interrogator. "When it suited her...The money she sent, how much could there have been? Enough for a little meat from the butcher? A Sunday sweet from the local pastry shop? Hardly compensation for your sacrifice."

"I never looked at it that way. Annette was caring and—"

"Never? Not in the dark of night as you sat alone in your tiny room? Did you not resent her freedom, her life in the City? How many times did you leave her from your prayers and curse her in the dark?"

The young woman lowered her eyes, and her chin came to rest on her chest. Gambrelli imagined that the tears were soon to come.

"When your mother finally died, was that not a secret relief to you? Did you wait an hour or a day before you began packing your things and planning to join Annette? Then when you arrived here, it was not what you had imagined, was it? Jobs were hard to find, many were without work. So you took a minor position in a dusty bookstore, carrying stacks of books with tattered covers, serving university students for a few pennies a day. Hardly the stuff dreams are made of."

The tears came. She searched her purse and pressed a handkerchief to her eyes.

"And while you were learning to accept your role, there in front of you every day was your sister. She had no trouble finding employment. First a well-paying job with the produce company, then a seemingly glamorous job at the Savage Gallery, surrounded by works of art, conversing with wealthy patrons. How many times did you cast an envious eye in her direction?"

Lisa turned her head to look at Detective Gavros.

"Look at me!" Gambrelli slammed his hand on the desk. "I am the one you will answer to." He stood up and leaned toward her. "Was it you, or Annette, who decided to steal the money from Gandone?"

She stared at Gambrelli, her lips trembling, her body twitching as if it was about to spring from the chair and flee. This time it was the chief inspector who glanced at the detectives. Bruno was impassive, his leathery eyelids concealing his mind; but young Gavros was wild-eyed, his mouth open about to cry out for Gambrelli to stop the attack.

"Annette told you where Gandone hid the cash. She told you it was behind the bookcase in the little room at the end of the narrow corridor."

"I didn't—"

"You cannot deny it. We have proof you were there."

"He's a liar," she screamed.

"Who is the liar? Valier?" Gambrelli walked around to her side of the desk. "No, we don't need his statement. We have scientific proof you were there." Again he looked at the two detectives. This time even Bruno's eyes betrayed disbelief.

Gambrelli hovered over the girl. For a moment he hesitated, knowing he was about to take a gamble he might not win. From the bag on his desk he removed the three rotted oranges supplied by Gandone.

"You see the grayish powder on these oranges? The police laboratory determined that it is a particular type of mold that grows only on the rind of the oranges from a specific grove located a few kilometers south of Valencia, Spain."

The young woman looked from the oranges to Gambrelli. Her face impassive, she waited for him to continue.

"You might find it interesting that Philippe Gandone is the only importer in the City who buys these oranges. His warehouse is the only place, south of Paris, where this precise mold may be found."

She lowered her eyes to the three oranges. Gambrelli could almost feel her mind churning in desperation as she came to the realization of what was to follow.

"We took the clothes from your apartment and had them examined by the police laboratory. On them were found traces of a gray powder. Actually, a powdered mold that is identical to the mold covering the crates of rotting oranges which line the sides of the narrow corridor in Gandone's warehouse." He picked up one of the oranges and shook it in her face. "This mold...none other."

She lowered her head. Her hands trembled. The gamble was won.

Gambrelli pressed on. "Now was it you, or Annette, or both of you who committed the theft?"

"I did it." She raised the handkerchief to her eyes.

"And Valier was your accomplice?"

"Yes." She bent her head into the small cloth and began to cry.

"Tell me all of it." Gambrelli's voice remained hard and demanding.

"I can't. I—"

"Your sister was murdered, and an innocent man has been killed, leaving a young family with no father. Two men have been arrested and may be executed for their part in these crimes." He pulled the handkerchief from her face. "You will tell it all, and you will tell it now."

She reached for her handkerchief, and Gambrelli threw it on the floor. She looked up at him. He showed her indifference. She bent to pick up the discarded cloth. He pushed her back into the chair. She wiped her eyes with her fingers, her nose and upper lip with the back of her hand.

"Annette told me about the money Gandone had hidden in the warehouse. We used to fantasize about stealing it. We called it our dowry. Annette would joke about it, but I treated it as real. Why not? Gandone had plenty of money. He could not report it to the police, because it was money he had made from smuggling. All I had to do was find a way into the warehouse."

She sat straight in the chair and looked directly at Gambrelli. Her eyes glistened, but he saw that her tears had been replaced with a blaze of defiance. He leaned back on the edge of the desk. He could relax. He knew the truth was about to be his.

"How did you recruit Valier?"

"It was simple: he is a man." She smiled at her inquisitor. "Annette introduced me to him at the market. We met him by accident, or so it seemed. I think now he must have been following her. In any event, it was clear he was infatuated with her. After Annette moved to the island and I decided to take the money, I followed Valier from his work to a café near Central Station. The rest was easy." Sometime during her confession, the smile had turned to a sneer.

"So it was you, not Annette, who planned the burglary."

"Annette? Please, Chief Inspector, Annette wouldn't pick up a coin from the street for concern that the one who dropped it would return looking for it." She pulled her hair back from her face. "Once I had the plan, I wrote Annette to tell her that I was going to collect our dowry. She returned to the City the night of the theft thinking she could stop me, but she was too late. By the time she reached the apartment on Leopold Street, it was done. All she could do was help me move to the new place. The next morning, she took the money and wrapped it in bundles so that I could hide it under the trap door in the closet."

"What of Valier? What was his share?"

"That is where the problems began." She rested her arms on her knees, appearing to talk directly to the front of Gambrelli's desk. "Annette had always said Gandone hid close to a million francs behind that shelf. I promised Valier one hundred and fifty thousand for his part."

"What was his part?"

"He was to let me in and make sure the night watchman didn't come around while I was there. That was all. One hundred and fifty thousand for that, can you imagine?" She shrugged at Gambrelli. "But when I counted the money, there was only four hundred thousand. Less than a half of what I'd expected. So I met with Valier the next day and told him he would have to settle for less."

"I can guess that was unacceptable to him." Gambrelli now took a tone of commiseration with her plight. "He took the same risk; regardless of the take, his contract was for a job which he completed."

"That's what he'd said. And truthfully, I couldn't argue the point. He'd also said he would rather kill me than settle for less."

"So you decided to stall him, buy some time to plan your escape, and cheat him out of his share. In spite of his threat, you decided to pay him nothing, right?"

"Exactly." She smiled a most charming smile.

"But you made the mistake of returning to the apartment on Leopold Street, and Valier was waiting for you."

"Yes, how did you—? No matter. He was there. I told him I was late for work and needed something from my apartment. He agreed to wait outside and then walk me to work so we could arrange for his payment. I took the opportunity to run out the back."

"When did you tell him Annette had the money?"

"The following day. He came upon me on the street. How he'd found me, I have no idea. Suddenly he was beside me, pushed me into an alleyway, and put a knife to my throat. He said he wanted his money. I told him Annette had taken it with her. When he asked where, I panicked. I didn't know what to say."

"That's when you told him Annette was living on the Island of Q?"

She nodded. "I told him Annette would be coming back on Friday with his share, and we could meet at the café near Central Station at two."

"And he believed you?" Gambrelli asked in disbelief.

"I told you he was a man, a lonely man. I gave him excuses and enough encouragement to believe me one more time." Gambrelli wasn't sure, but he thought a slight blush crossed her cheeks. He looked at Gavros. The youthful face of the detective was unmistakably red.

"And when you did not make the meeting on Friday, did you not suspect he would set out to find Annette?"

"No. I'd assumed he would go to the house on Leopold. Since no one knew where I had gone, and I had stopped working at the bookstore, there was no way for him to find me. I thought I could warn Annette, convince her to return to our hometown where we would be safe."

"But Valier cut short that plan when he cut your sister's throat," Gambrelli said with an exaggerated casualness.

Lisa Cuomo fell silent.

Gambrelli looked at the two detectives and spoke with resignation, "Bruno, take her to the matrons at the fortress. I want her in a cell alone. Tell them to keep a watch on her."

Detective Gavros waited at the edge of Gambrelli's desk until Lisa's and Bruno's footsteps faded down the hall.

"Even without the confession, she would have had a difficult time explaining the mold on her clothing," Gavros said pointing to the oranges.

"Yes that would have been damning to her case...Especially if it were true."

The detective was speechless. He stared at the chief inspector for several moments before the reality of Gambrelli's ploy settled in his mind.

"What made you suspect her?" Gavros asked in a subdued tone.

Gambrelli had been asked that question many times over the years. His standard reply was a shrug and a wave of the hand as if to say, "*Dieu seul le sait.*" God only knows. This time he stopped halfway through the shrug. Something in the young detective's eyes made him pause. It was not just curiosity, but perhaps a desire to understand.

"There may have been things I saw, or heard that entered my mind without my knowing...but the first I can recall was when we told her Bertrand had been arrested. It struck me that her declaration of Bertrand's innocence was...too immediate...too certain."

"That's all, that was it?"

"The rest is in the reports." He looked at Gavros' bewildered expression and decided to continue for a moment longer.

"Nothing really occurred to me until I gave thought to the night in her apartment." He looked hard at Gavros. "As Valier stood over Lisa's bed, thinking her beneath the covers, he said that she had cheated him." Gambrelli paused. When a glimmer of understanding crossed the young man's face he continued, "A few moments later she took the gun from your waistband... It would have been a simple matter for her to shoot Escobar... He was standing just to her left. Instead, she lunged forward, thrusting the gun past your attempts to block her. She fired across the room at Valier. Then she screamed, 'He murdered my sister.' Remember?"

"But it *was* Valier who killed her sister."

"We know that now, but how could she know it then? Only if she knew Valier was the murderer would she have risked all to kill him."

The detective understood. "Kill him for revenge, or to silence him, or both."

"That was my thought," Gambrelli said. "In any event, there was no doubt that she was involved in the chain of events leading to her sister's murder. Since then it has been a matter of determining how and to what extent."

"About the gun she took from me, I assume there will be a full inquiry and discipline against me." Gavros stood rigid, hands behind his back as if awaiting the impact of bullets from a firing squad.

"There will be no inquiry."

"But regulations require—"

"I decide what is required in this bureau." Gambrelli pulled himself to his full height and look down into the young detective's eyes. "If there is another incident of that type, you will be dismissed from the Major Crimes Bureau without a recommendation for retention in the Investigations Division.

"Now go and prepare a report on the girl's statements. When Bruno returns, he can help you recall the details. I will be back in an hour. Make sure the report is ready."

THIRTY-FIVE

The Saturday afternoon bartender at the Watchman's Tavern stood at the end of the bar
polishing glasses. He had been a patrol sergeant in
the Harbor District when Gambrelli had been assigned there as a new inspector. His attempts to
reminisce about old friends and cases with the chief
inspector had gone poorly, so the former sergeant
gave up and concentrated on his task, holding each
glass up to the light to examine the results of his
efforts.

The waitress set a plate of sliced dried sausages
and cheese next to Gambrelli's half-finished glass
of beer. "Another?" She pointed to the glass, resting
the side of her left breast against his arm.

"In a minute," he said, ignoring her attempt to
encourage his consumption. He was annoyed that
he had not pushed on with Lisa Cuomo. He had
wanted her to admit that she coveted her sister's
lover—that she had planned to seduce Bertrand.

And why not? He couldn't blame her for trying. Bertrand was a man of means. He could easily afford to contribute to the welfare of two women who were practically the mirror image of each other. One for the city, and one for the island.

"Of all the thoughts to have come to my mind..." He sipped the beer and put a slice of rosette de ville and cheese on the crusty bread.

"What did you say?" The barman was encouraged.

"Nothing, I was just thinking that I have gotten into the habit of wanting to know everything about a case, even things that are of no consequence to the matter at hand."

"You were always like that." The barman set down a glass and slung the towel over his shoulder. "Ever since your first day in the district, you were like that, always poking for the last bit of information."

"Was I?" Gambrelli said with genuine interest as he took a sip of beer.

"As I remember, every time someone was brought in, you would ask them a hundred questions. Even after they confessed, you were still at it: 'When did you commit your first crime? How did it make you feel? Did you get along well with your father, your mother, your classmates?' I swear you drove them all crazy with your questioning."

"I was trying to learn..." Gambrelli started in his own defense.

"You were a pain in the ass. Probably still are."
The barman laughed and slapped Gambrelli on the
shoulder.

"You are quite right, Sergeant. I most certainly
am." The chief inspector laughed and took a bite of
bread and sausage.

His mouth was full and the crust of the bread
was cutting into his palate when Sergeant Andres
and Inspector Renard entered the tavern. They
took their usual seats at the end of the bar next to
Gambrelli.

"So the girl's been arrested?" Andres asked.

"She's locked up for the night. If the prosecutors
choose to pursue charges, so be it. If not, what does
it matter to us?" Gambrelli ran his tongue back and
forth along the roof of his mouth, tasting for blood
before taking another bite.

"The reports on Ferris are on your desk,"
Renard said while pointing to Gambrelli's beer, indicating to the barman to bring three of the same.

"No more for me." Gambrelli waved a hand
over the top of his glass. "We will need to follow up
on the Ferris murder. Perhaps there will be enough
to charge Valier." To Andres he added, "Tomorrow,
begin the interview of the neighbors, maybe someone other than Ferris' six year old daughter saw
Valier drive him off that night."

"There are a lot of houses on that street," Andres said.

"Use as many men as you need, but get it done
quickly. If we can file charges on Valier before Major

Ormond transports him to the island on Monday it would be best."

Renard swallowed his first sip of beer. "We can start tonight."

"Even better, but tomorrow Renard, I want you to obtain warrants for a search of Valier's home and any locker at the warehouse he may use to store his personal effects. We will need to find the weapon he used to kill Ferris. I will notify the police surgeon to immediately conduct an autopsy of Ferris and have a general description of the weapon used in the crime.

"Ask him to have someone available to check whatever we find for traces of Ferris' blood."

For a few minutes they were quiet, turning their attention to the bread, sausages and cheese. The waitress again came to Gambrelli's elbow.

"Are you sure you wouldn't like another Chief Inspector?"

He resisted the temptation. "Not now, but bring us a plate of roasted garlic sausage."

"So Renard, you've offered to help me with interviews tonight, but I thought Saturday nights you head to the races?"

"I don't bet anymore in September."

"I thought the Lenten season was your only time of rest." Gambrelli poked at Andres's arm.

"In my maturity, I have also added the thirty days of September to my traditional forty." Renard waited for his companions to stop grinning. "I put the money I would have bet this month in a jar in my kitchen, until the first Saturday in October."

"And then what? Pass it on to the sisters of charity at the hospital?" Andres laughed and returned a poke to Gambrelli's arm.

Renard leaned toward them and dropped his voice to a whisper. "The first Saturday in October, they have a couple of 'get even' races for the regulars." He winked.

"You mean fixed races?" Gambrelli made no attempt to lower his voice.

"Not really fixed... I mean anything can happen... but things are arranged to give a few of us a better chance of guessing the outcome." Renard gave another wink before taking a long drink.

Gambrelli pushed the small platter of meats and cheese toward his men and patted them on the back. "Good work these few days." On his way out the door he called to the waitress, "Put their check on my account."

· · ·

At two-forty-five, Detective Bruno walked into the chief's office and placed several sheets of paper on the desk.

"It's a little brief, but all the essential facts are in it." Bruno sat opposite Gambrelli. "Gavros had most of it done when I got back from signing the girl into the fortress."

"Where is he now?"

"He said he was going out to get some air. I think the turn in the girl's story shook him a little."

Gambrelli did not reply. He scanned the report then did the same to the one written by Andres and Renard. He was just finishing when Chief Superintendent Wilhelm walked in. The superintendent swaggered forward, the brass buttons of his dress uniform sparkling. Even Gambrelli was momentarily impressed.

"Here's your file, Gambrelli." He dropped it on the corner of the desk and turned to walk away.

"There are some additional reports for you to read." Gambrelli held up the documents completed that afternoon.

"I don't have time now. My press conference begins in less than an hour. I'll read them later."

"I would suggest you read them now. There are—"

"Later, Gambrelli," Wilhelm said over his shoulder as he stepped into the hall.

"Then at least let me explain—"

"If I want to hear anything more from you I will let you know." Wilhelm marched away.

Gambrelli tried not to smile, but the effort was in vain. "Detective Bruno, I want it remembered that I attempted to provide Chief Superintendent Wilhelm with the completed investigative files."

"I am a witness." Bruno said without repressing his grin.

"And that I offered to bring him up to date verbally."

"You did, I heard you."

"And this final effort was prior to his public statements."

"It was, one hour before." Bruno checked his watch.

"Isn't Lanier due in at four?" He changed the subject as his urge to smile faded.

"I'm working for him tonight. It's his kid's birthday," Bruno said. "He'll be in tomorrow morning."

"Good. I want you and Lanier to help Sergeant Andres with some door to door interviews. But before that go to the fortress and get a formal statement from Lisa Cuomo. I want everything she can recall: dates, times, locations...From the moment she decided to rob Gandone...everything related to her actions in concert with Valier."

"I can do it now."

"No, I want her to spend the night in jail. Give her a taste of what may be in store."

"Should I take Lanier with me, as a witness?"

"That would be best." Gambrelli picked up the papers on his desk.

"Do you want me to take that file to the duty prosecutor's office?"

"No, I'll take care of it. Renard and Andres are at the Watchman. Go join them. When I see Gavros, I'll send him over," he said as he inserted the day's reports into the Annette Cuomo file.

THIRTY-SIX

Gambrelli passed no one in the marble halls of the Palais de Justice which seemed to him more like a mausoleum than usual. He tried to quiet the sound of his footsteps then realized there was no one to be disturbed.

He was certain the duty magistrate, Paul Neulon, had been sleeping when he entered the cluttered office without knocking. To Gambrelli it was almost to be expected that a man nearer to eighty than seventy should be napping on a quite Saturday afternoon. In fact had he consumed another beer he might be dozing as well.

"Chief Inspector, a surprise to see you," the magistrate said, busying himself by moving papers from his left to his right and back again.

"Monsieur le Judge, I've brought the file on the Annette Cuomo murder."

"Ah, the Bertrand matter. Let me see it." The magistrate extended a thin-fingered hand. Gambrelli noticed the man's fingernails were exceedingly long and in need of cleaning.

He released the file into the emaciated grasp of the magistrate, and the packet hit the desk with a thud as if it had been dropped.

"Sorry," Gambrelli said, "I thought you had hold of it."

Gambrelli had known Judge Neulon for decades. Even when the man was fit he would labor for an hour over reports any of the other magistrates could read in a fourth the time. Hoping not to fall asleep Gambrelli remained standing. After a few minutes he found himself leaning against the window frame watching the barges tied along the river bank.

Absently he began to replay Marie's narration of her day in the park with Odin and the rescue of the boy Jules.

"Have you ever noticed how he stands between me and whomever I am talking to?" She had asked. "No I don't suppose you have...since he only does it when you are not there...That's his way of protecting me...He never does that with you? Does he? Probably not...he knows you can take care of yourself..."

Gambrelli started to think. Did the dog ever become a protective barrier for him. The other day when talking to Monsieur Mordant...Was Odin standing between them? He didn't think so. Did he ever? Gambrelli thought 'maybe'. He swore to take note of the dog's actions in the future.

From there his mind drifted to Sergeant Andres' recent tendency to inquire about his health... and the other night his men were overly concerned with leaving their boss in Lisa Cuomo's apartment to wait alone for the suspects. First his detectives... Now his dog...

"Do they all think I've gone over the hill?"

"Excuse me Chief Inspector, what did you say?"

Gambrelli turned and looked around the room, not quite sure of where he was.

"Nothing, Monsieur le Judge, I was just thinking out loud."

"Terrible business, this," the magistrate said, closing the file, apparently accustomed to disregarding the mumblings of day dreaming visitors. "Has the judge on the island reviewed these reports?"

"No, they will be sent with the prisoners on Monday."

"And what is to be done with the woman, Lisa Cuomo."

"She is in custody."

"To be charged with what?"

"Maybe nothing."

"But she is in jail...we must have a reason."

"Protective custody will do for now. We still don't know if others were involved in her sister's murder."

"I can live with that, but no longer than Monday. Then she must be formally arrested with a warrant or released. Am I clear on that?"

"Monday will be long enough for us to clear things up…one way or the other."

Neulon gathered up the reports and placed them in the file envelope.

"I can pass this to the prosecutor, if you like."

"Those are for you. I have others."

"Jean Michel Bertrand is a good man." He looked up at Gambrelli, as if awaiting concurrence.

Silence.

"I said Bertrand is a good man."

"I heard you."

"Well he's a damn fine prosecutor."

"He'll probably be even better now," Gambrelli said.

"What makes you say that?"

"He's had a good taste of the other side."

·   ·   ·

Gambrelli retraced his path to Police Headquarters, where reporters were gathering in the lobby of the new wing. Slightly elevated above the crowd was Chief Superintendent Wilhelm, waiting for the reporters to settle before beginning his statement. As Gambrelli made his way along the back of the group, his progress was halted by Gandone's attorney, Malbec.

"Looks like I made it just in time," Malbec said.

Gambrelli pushed past him.

"Gandone said you wanted me here." Malbec pulled on Gambrelli's sleeve, his breath smelling of wine.

"Stay, go, do as you like. My advice would be to shut up and listen to what is to be said." He pulled his arm free. "And never speak to me again unless I acknowledge you first."

. . .

Returning to the Major Crimes Bureau, Gambrelli looked into the detectives' bay. Detective Gavros was alone, standing in the middle of the room.

"Gavros."

"Chief."

"The men are across the street. Go join them for a drink. You've earned it."

"You think so?" He sat on a bench near the large stove. "I don't."

Gambrelli paced in front of the stove, rubbing his hand against the stubble on his chin, searching for the right words.

"Every investigation has something to teach us, lad. The good cases have many points of instruction." He looked at Gavros, who was staring at the floor. "This has been a good case, Gavros. We can all learn from it. Not just about methods of investigation, but about ourselves. When the file is returned from the prosecutor's office, I want you to take it and read it through." Gavros was looking at him now. "Talk about it with the other men."

"I couldn't. They saw me with her. They will have a great laugh on the junior man."

"Do you think you are the first who has been blinded by a beautiful woman?"

"But we are policemen."

"All the more reason." Gambrelli put a foot up on the bench and rested his forearms on his knee. "As a matter of course, we only see people in crisis. In our business, when we meet a woman, she is truly a damsel in distress, and we are destined for the role of the knight, sworn by his honor, to save her from harm." Gambrelli stopped himself before he went any further. "The others may ride you tonight, but know that every one of us has played the same role before."

"Even you, Chief?"

"More than the rest of you put together." Gambrelli patted the young man on the shoulder. "Now go across the street and join your comrades."

THIRTY-SEVEN

He was following Madame Gambrelli to the top of the stairs when the phone in the parlor rang.

"Go on to bed," he said. "I'll get it."

He forced himself down the stairs. The mantel clock read nine-thirty. He answered the phone. It was Sergeant Andres.

"Did I wake you?"

"Would you be happier if you had?" He took a cigarette from a silver box and began searching his robe for a match.

"We just got a call from the shift lieutenant in the University District. Another woman has been murdered."

Silence, then a grunt, followed by an exhaling of air that was almost a sigh.

"The body was discovered in her apartment by a roommate about thirty minutes ago. The lieutenant said it looks like the same method as was used in the killing last month. He asked if we wanted to send someone to the scene."

"Who have you got?"

"Just me and Detective Bruno."

"Send Bruno. Tell him he is to observe only. Let the district detectives handle it. We can review their reports later."

"I can go with him in case—"

"No. Go home and get some rest. Bruno will be fine. He can call you if there is anything to report." Gambrelli gave up his search for a match and returned the cigarette to the box.

At the top of the stairs, he held on to the wooden globe atop the newel and leaned heavily against the post. In the silence, he could hear the wind and the rain. He was tired. His shoulder ached from the dampness. There was a pain in the center of his back and in his hip.

Odin was standing on the landing staring at him. For a moment, he felt panic and was under the impression that he had stopped breathing. He couldn't remember when he had taken his last breath. Suffocating, drowning, he gasped and inhaled deeply.

"Arthur, are you all right?" Marie called from the bedroom.

He walked slowly toward her voice and leaned on the doorframe of the darkened bedroom. The dog stood by his side. He patted the furry head.

"I'm fine, just tired."

"Was the call from Headquarters?"

"Yes, Sergeant Andres."

"Is there a problem?"

"No, it was nothing."

"Then come to bed, Artu. Let us listen to the rain."

THE END

CPSIA information can be obtained at www.ICGtesting.com
Printed in the USA
LVOW04s0240310815

452162LV00032B/1022/P